Jamison

CHRIS
KENISTON
USA TODAY BESTSELLING AUTHOR

Indie House Publishing

Indie House Publishing

BOOKS BY CHRIS KENISTON

Sweet Aloha Series

Aloha Texas

Almost Paradise

Mai Tai Marriage

Dive Into You

Shell Game

Look of Love

Love by Design

Love Walks In

Surf's Up Flirts

(Aloha Series Companions)

Shall We Dance

Love on Tap

Head Over Heels

Perfect Match

Just One Kiss

It Had to Be You

Honeymoon Series

Honeymoon for One

Honeymoon for Three

Family Secrets Novels

Champagne Sisterhood

The Homecoming

Hope's Corner

Farraday Country

Adam

Brooks

Connor

Declan

Ethan

Finn

Grace

Hannah

Ian

Jamison

Keeping Eileen

ACKNOWLEDGEMENTS

Between *Ian* and *Jamison* my daughter got married, I wound up on crutches, and I still have the best writing friends in the world. Frankly, I don't know where this series would be without the quirky ideas of Cindy Dees. She might write suspense but she's a well of fun ideas for Farraday Country. Kathy Ivan, Barbara Han, Linda Steinberg, and Kellie Coates Gilbert are always just a phone call or Chinese dinner away when I find myself falling off track. Thank you all ! Special shout out to my hubby Paul who does his best to protect my writing time and sing my praises whether folks want to read romance or not – lol. Love you bunches. And thank you to all my readers – you make writing Farraday Country fun!

CHAPTER ONE

Timing was everything, and now was the time.

Scattered pieces of crumbling construction, dust, mildew and old age mingled, creating the sweetest smell on earth. Jamison Farraday squeezed the keys to the ancient building in his hand—an establishment all his own. Well, not exactly his, but he would be the general manager. The concept, the research, the plans, those were all his. Fed and nurtured by years of observing, learning, working, and saving. Financed by one of the more successful conglomerates in the bar and nightclub industry.

"Are you sure about this?" Ian, his brother, and DJ, his cousin, swatted their arms, cutting through dangling cobwebs, making their way across the abandoned storefront.

"Never been more sure of anything in my life."

Ian smiled at his older brother. "Anyone else and I'd have said you lost your mind, but I'm guessing this won't be the last time you prove us short-sighted mortals wrong."

Having the support of his family was probably the best reason he'd dared to dream, taken chances, worked his butt off at every job in the business until he was sure he could pull of his big dream. A family style Irish pub.

"You do know that Mabel Berkner is already starting up a petition to appeal the vote to sell liquor in this county." DJ brushed the dust from his hands. "Not that she's going to get very far with it, but she's not the only one in town with ruffled feathers over this."

"I expected a little flack, but by the time we're ready and open for business and the crime rate doesn't skyrocket overnight due to," Jamison put on a thick southern accent, "our *vile influence*, everyone will settle down and get back to the business of ordinary living."

"So what exactly is the plan?" Walking about, DJ eyed the exposed rafters.

"The architect we chose for the project is putting the most recent changes on paper. Final plans should be ready any day now. With plan approval in hand, the money men will take on the next step after the letter of intent and ink the final contract with Mr. Thomas. Then we'll be down to a few more weeks for the title company to do their magic. I can hardly wait to get a crew in here. Clean it out and rebuild."

"I can see it." Ian stood in place, looking around and nodding. "I really can. Knotty pine walls?"

Jamie bobbed his head.

"Dance floor?" DJ asked.

Again, Jamie nodded. His smile pulling tighter against his cheeks. He had it all worked out. Including having lined up some of the best craft beers in Texas. One company on the verge of expanding even talked of growing out here, away from the overcrowded city.

The corners of Ian's mouth tipped skyward, exposing the dimples the girls always gushed over. "Irish music?"

"Oh yeah." Jamie grinned back at his brother.

DJ chuckled. "If that doesn't have Uncle Brian here every weekend crooning with Dad, Saint Patrick isn't Irish."

"I'm counting on more folks than Dad feeling that way." Jamison slapped his cousin on the back. "I wish all the legal stuff were over and done. I've been itching to get working on this place for months and now it's all so close."

"Overseeing concept, design, and now construction before the doors even open. Sounds like you're going to be wearing an awful lot of hats on this project." Adam Farraday crossed the threshold. "On my way back to the clinic and I saw the door open. Y'all throwing a party without me?"

"Wouldn't think of it," Jamie answered, glancing down at the express mail tube in his cousin's arm. "What's that?"

“Oh, Maggie at the post office asked me to give this to you.”

“The plans.” Jamie couldn’t get the container open fast enough.

Adam stood shoulder to shoulder with his brother. “For this place?”

“Yes.” Jamie squatted on the ground and unrolled the large pages.

His brother hovered behind him. “Why didn’t they just email them?”

“I don’t know.” Jamie studied the architectural rendering. “That’s what I was expecting.”

“You’re frowning.” Ian inched closer. “What is it?”

Jamie shook his head. He had to be looking at the wrong plans. Turning the page, he scooted around to align the front of the store with the top of the plans. There was no mistaking what he saw. Nothing was laid out the way the planning committee and the architect had originally discussed, the way he and the backers had agreed. “This doesn’t even look like a pub.” He pointed to the back section of the drawing. “This should be the dance floor.”

“I’m not an architect,” DJ leaned forward more, “but there doesn’t seem to be anything remotely like a dance floor on that page anywhere.”

“That’s because there isn’t. What should be space for a little boot scooting is an open kitchen.” Jaimie had worked enough bars and restaurants to know the concept and recognize it on paper. He looked to the corner of the drawings. Above the architect’s scales and name was the street address and town for the project. Correct. The establishment not so much. Not a pub. Not his pub. Hemingway’s International Grill. What the …

“From the look on your face,” Ian stretched upright, “I gather this is news to you?”

Jamie stabbed at his phone, held it to his ear and nodded.

“Is it that bad?” Ian asked.

“International grill,” Jamie muttered. “This town is no place for a chain restaurant.”

DJ looked from his cousin to his brother. “I suppose that’s no worse than Irish.”

“Seriously?” Jamie stared at his cousin. Before he could say another word, voice mail kicked in. “Thank you for calling Crocker International—”

“Like Betty Crocker?” Ian asked wide-eyed.

Jamie shook his head and mumbled, “No relation.” The recording came to an end and the beep signaled his turn to talk. He’d have much preferred speaking to Jeff Nimbus in person, but this would have to do. “Jeff, Jamison Farraday here. Just received the blueprints for The Public House and they’re marked Hemingway’s. Give me a call when you have a minute.”

“Don’t bite my head off,” Ian held a hand out at him, “but is there a reason an Irish pub is better suited to this town than an international grill?”

“An Irish pub is basically Abbie’s small town café with an accent. And in our case, local wine, maybe if all goes well, beer, and of course dancing. Pubs are neighborhood watering holes. People know each other. Men have a drink and tell stories that have been handed down for ages. Young and old gather.”

“He has a point.” Adam shrugged. “Except for the booze and dancing, it sounds an awful lot like the café.”

“Of course I have a point. Every small town in Ireland has and supports its own pub. The same would be true here, except Tuckers Bluff isn’t so small anymore, we’re growing.”

“With all the advertising the county’s been doing for the ghost town circuit, the vineyard the Brady’s have been working, and a hospital in town, we’re growing faster than any other small town in West Texas. And mark my words, if given a choice, folks living halfway to Butler Springs will want to come here to the pub for some dancing and a drink or two rather than go all the way to Butler Springs for the same old same old.”

DJ hooked his hand around the back of his neck. “I’ll admit, if international is code word for fancy and expensive, then Jamie’s right. Folks won’t be banging down the doors.”

"It's worse than that." Jamie raked his fingers through his hair and then hung his hand along the back of his neck. "Can you see the fine citizens of Tuckers Bluff eating sushi?"

"Sushi?" Adam's forehead folded into layers. "What does Hemingway have to do with sushi?"

"The man, nothing, but the restaurant serves everything trendy. They're based in California and last year spread their wings to Austin and Dallas. They cater to urban millennials." In his shirt pocket, his phone buzzed. Recognizing the number, DJ was surprised to get a response from Nimbus so quickly. "Hello."

"Hey, was on a conference call. Isn't it great news?"

"Great news?"

"Yes. Babcock Foods wants in. We negotiated a sweet deal. Hemingway's is all the rage."

"In LA, sure. Maybe even Dallas, but it's not a fit for West Texas."

"Nonsense. Our research shows—"

"You mean my research."

"No, Jamison. Our merchandising department ran some backup market analysis. The pub idea is good."

Better than good, but no point repeating that now.

"And without Babcock Foods, we would have followed through. But Babcock has very deep pockets and this is the perfect alliance for Crocker to branch out to the restaurant side of the industry. If Babcock wants Hemingway's in Tuckers Bluff, they're going to get it."

This wasn't good. "Someone needs to explain to the board that this is not the time to—"

"It's a done deal, Jamie. There's no explaining. Come Monday, the final papers will be signed. The question is, do you still want to be a part of this?"

• • • •

Standing on her feet from dawn to dusk, and then some, was Abbie's reality. One she and her painfully expensive shoes had made peace with a very long time ago.

"Here, drink this." Frank, the cook, slid a warm mug in front of her. "It won't do much for your feet, but it will help your mood." One corner of the man's mouth tilted up in a cheeky grin. "I put some of your special stash in it."

She kept a bottle of Bailey's under the counter for the occasional customer who needed a little something extra in their coffee after an especially rough day. Or night. She didn't care much for the taste of it herself unless it was buried deep in something chocolaty, but Frank knew that. The something special wouldn't equate to much more than a splash. His desired intent accomplished. To make her smile.

Looking out for her had become a regular part of Frank's routine through the years. Some days she didn't need looking after as much as others, but she always appreciated it, appreciated him. Another slow sip of the chocolaty brew slid all the way down to her toes. "Just what I needed."

"What you need," Frank stepped back and took his place behind the grill, "is a day off. A real day off. Or two."

This wasn't the first nor the last time she expected to hear the same advice. "You sound like a broken record."

"That doesn't make it any less true."

"Would that be the pot calling the kettle black?" The man worked every shift right alongside her. She'd tried hiring a part time cook to give Frank a break, but the sour Marine became surlier than ever. In the end he once again became ruler supreme of his kitchen kingdom.

Reluctant to set the mug down, she took another sip, lingering in the relaxation a moment longer. The dinner rush would be picking up soon and as good as Shannon, the evening shift waitress, was at her job, Abbie needed to get out of the kitchen and do her share.

"You're worried, aren't you?" Plating an order, Frank didn't bother to look up.

She blew on the warm liquid even though it was no longer that hot. “What’s there to worry about?”

“You could get a liquor license too.”

“This is a café, not a night club.” Besides, rumor had it the town council was considering limiting the number of liquor licenses to keep Mabel Berkner happy. That woman’s devotion to a dry county would have made her temperance ancestors very proud.

“A dance floor wouldn’t hurt. A small one.” He rang the bell for Shannon to pick up her order.

They’d had this conversation before as well. The first time had been back when word got about that a new supper club was considering setting up here in town. Then the conversation resumed when the referendum came about to change Tuckers Bluff from a dry to wet town, making the county more appealing to competition. Worried or not, either way, her mind was set about not changing the cafe. Pushing away from the stainless prep area she’d been leaning against, she blew out a short breath. If only she could expel life’s aggravations as easily. “I’ll take that out.”

Lifting his chin to see over the shiny metal on deck shelf in front of him, Frank leveled his gaze with hers but didn’t say another word. He didn’t have to. She could see the worry in his eyes. Not that he had any reason to. Today was no different than any other day over the years. Except he was right about one thing. She was tired. Not just from working six and a half days a week, every week, but the kind of tired that stopped a heart from dreaming, and after all these years, she wanted to dream again.

• • • •

“I’ll be honest.” Jamie’s Uncle Sean rubbed at his chin. “Never understood why you’d want to take an idea you are so sure of, do the brunt of the work for, and let someone else reap most of the benefits.”

"That's easy." Catherine, his cousin Connor's wife, chimed in. "Money. Building out a restaurant where there wasn't one before is an extremely expensive venture. Then you have to squirrel away the funds to run the operation for at least six months while the patronage grows enough to support the business, never mind make a profit. A year would be even better. And then, in this case, include the purchase of real estate involved, well…"

"How much money are we talking?" His cousin Finn, the youngest of the West Texas Farraday brothers, dropped his ankle over his knee and took a sip of his beer.

"No." Jamie skipped over answering the original question and jumped straight to the next one he knew would be coming. No matter how confident he was, he would not put his family's money at risk. It's why he hadn't said anything to his West Texas kin until the deal was an inch from signed, sealed and delivered.

"No money involved?" Finn's wife Joanna took a seat on the arm of her husband's chair and grinned up at Jamie. A full-time writer, the woman had an interesting sense of humor—and irony—and could tease and rag on the family as good as the members born into the Farraday clan.

Aunt Eileen stood up from her spot on the sofa beside his uncle and moved to the ottoman alongside Jamie. When his aunt got that determined look in her eye, he knew the chances of walking through a cow pen on shipping day without stepping on a paddy were greater than withstanding Force Eileen.

Glancing around the room of relatives, it dawned on him that almost everyone had that same expression painted on their faces. Whether they'd been born a Farraday or married one. He should have realized when his cousins from town and their spouses had shown up for a family supper in the middle of the week that there was more to the visit than hot food and a little moral support. Something else was brewing.

Aunt Eileen set her hand on his forearm. "We've been talking."

"When?" Except for the time it took to drive from town to the ranch, Jamie had been with his aunt and uncle all evening.

She shrugged. "I suppose the conversation started back when you first mentioned bringing a pub to Tuckers Bluff."

"Thought you'd lost your mind." Uncle Sean chuckled. "Then I started listening a little more closely to the conversations around town. Paying attention to exactly how many folks go driving to Butler Springs for a special dinner or a little Friday night shuffle. More than I'd realized, I'll tell you that."

Aunt Eileen rolled her eyes at her brother-in-law. "Just cause you're a homebody doesn't mean the rest of the world is."

"Since when is being a family man a bad thing?" Uncle Sean's brow knit together.

"Even family men are allowed to get out of the house once in a while."

"I get out."

Waving a finger at her brother-in-law, Aunt Eileen's mouth dropped open. "The barn isn't considered—"

A loud whistle pierced the air cutting off conversation. Finn's fingers slid away from his lips. "Can we focus please?"

Meg, Adam's wife, flashed a broad approving grin at Finn before picking up the dropped thread of conversation. "Look at Friday Girls' Night. We not only spend money for food or entertainment if we go to Butler Springs, we spend a ton on gas too. Just saving money on driving, never mind the time, would bring an awful lot of folks to a new night spot."

DJ leaned forward, resting his forearms on his knees. "I'll admit I've been a bit concerned over what this would mean for Abbie. Frankly, I think she's a little worried too, though she won't admit it. But Dad's right. This town and folks nearby spend a lot of money trucking all the way to Butler Springs. As long as the place is different from what Abbie offers, I think we can handle two choices for dinner."

"What about lunch?" Becky, DJ's wife, asked.

Jamie shook his head. "Not practical." Though with the new direction Crocker wanted to take, he had no idea what the group's intentions were anymore.

"You're frowning." Aunt Eileen's brows buckled to match his. "What are you thinking?"

His recent concerns over the impact of Crocker's possible new plans wasn't something he wanted to expand on just yet. At this point he needed to focus on what he knew would work. "To start, the pub would be open for long weekends only. Thursday through Sunday. No lunch. No hard impact on the café."

He didn't have to say anything else. Several men cut from the same gene pool shifted forward or back, but all grit their teeth and nodded.

DJ sucked in a long breath. "And there are no guarantees what the backers will do now?"

Jamie shook his head. He should have known better than to assume he'd be the only one in the room to put the pieces together. "If they're not following through on the deal as originally planned, there's no telling what else they will, or won't, do."

"I'm not in the real estate or restaurant business," Uncle Sean looked to his nephew, "but that building has been an eye sore on this town, sitting empty ever since the feed store expanded across the street almost two decades ago. Not many people have a need for a place that size and old Jake Thomas asked a king's ransom of anyone who showed interest. The way I see it, he wasn't at all serious about selling till you brought a deal to the table."

There was a grain of truth in what his uncle said. Jamie knew for a fact that there was a sense of owing the Farradays a debt for standing behind his son in an effort to keep him out of jail. Not that Jamie had been all that sure it wasn't more a matter of timing, wanting all his business deals off his hands, the way he'd sold the feed store to Grace's husband. Regardless, whatever the reason for the old man's change of heart, Jamie was kicking up his heels. Or had been.

"Actually," Adam spoke up, "there's a rumor going around that without Farraday involvement, the old man won't sell."

That had Jamie's ears perking up. "Where'd you hear that?"

Grace's husband, Chase, smiled and raised one finger. "I may have planted a seed or two when I spoke with Jake this afternoon. Mentioned that I could see where it would have disturbed him to hear Jamie is considering stepping out of the project. The words *the new plans were doomed to fail* might have been mentioned, along with *folks are slow to trust strangers around here without someone from town to back them up*."

"Not bad, hubby." Grace leaned over and kissed Chase on the cheek. She, like Jamie, knew that the deal struck by Crocker was a lower point of sale with a profit percentage over time. "Not bad at all."

"Hey," he ran the back of his knuckles along her chin, "I may have given up life on Wall Street, but that doesn't mean I've forgotten how to play the game."

Game. Could he even consider what his family was setting up for him? Buy the place himself? Single and simple living had allowed him to stash some money. Nothing near enough for an investment like this on his own or he wouldn't have settled for general manager to a company with Crocker's track record. He'd dismissed business loans as an option. The kind of money he'd need, loans could be crippling when it came to getting the business off the ground. And even if he were willing to take the risk, he'd need more collateral. And that he didn't have.

"Did you know old man Thomas carried the note for me when I bought the feed store?"

"I'd bet with the building as collateral banks would be willing to lend the money for the remodel," Meg volunteered. "I may even still have a few connections that can help."

He'd forgotten she used to run a boutique hotel and restaurant when she lived in Dallas. Still, the whole idea was simply crazy. Even with his savings and some good connections, with a note attached, the building wouldn't be very attractive as collateral.

"Well, I think investing in this town is a smart idea." Uncle Sean skewered his nephew with a stern glare. "I'd be willing to kick in for a share of the building, and I'm thinking so would your dad."

A few voices tumbled over each other with comments along the lines of they each had money just burning a hole in their pocket. He knew they weren't lying. He had savings as well and banks paid miserable interest rates. He also knew that risking their life's savings wasn't the Farraday way.

"And before you go thinking this is some silly whim," Uncle Sean waved a finger at him, "there's a condition attached."

"Condition?" He hadn't even agreed to let the family help and his uncle was already talking conditions.

"Let me guess." Adam looked to his dad. "You want the place called Farradays."

"Well, it does make sense," Aunt Eileen almost scolded her oldest nephew.

"Actually," Uncle Sean spoke directly to Jamie, "a good Irish pub needs a good Irish name."

"Farraday's isn't Irish?" Aunt Eileen muttered.

"I was thinking something a bit older than that," Uncle Sean leaned forward, "O'Fearadaigh's."

CHAPTER TWO

"You really are going to do it." Abbie passed through the open doors into the vacant storefront, Frank on her heels.

"Entering enemy territory?" Maneuvering over an old broken bench, Jamie inched forward. "Watch your step. This place is one giant booby trap."

"No kidding." She honed in on the ancient cash register sitting on what was left of a counter. "Oh, wow. I haven't seen anything like that outside of photographs."

"Works too." Jamie flashed that same photogenic smile every Farraday possessed.

"Of course it does." Standing beside the register, she ran her fingers along the dusty ornate trim, then pushed a button. The bell clanged and the drawer popped open. "These suckers were manufactured before planned obsolescence."

Frank scanned the rear, inching his way in that direction. "It's bigger than it appears from the outside. Mind if I take a closer look?"

"Recognizance?" Jamie laughed at Frank's scowl. "Go ahead, but be careful. There are a lot of surprises everywhere."

The moment the last café customer had paid the tab, Frank mentioned Jamie was in town at the vacant site and suggested they come check the place out. Abbie hadn't needed much convincing, her curiosity was driving her to distraction. "Didn't expect to see you here on a Sunday afternoon. Your Aunt Eileen can't be too happy if you're missing supper."

Jamie tapped some papers sticking out of his shirt pocket. "Special dispensation."

"Everyone's talking about your plans to buy the building

yourself. Word must have spread through church this morning faster than the sermon put folks to sleep."

"Not a plan." He tapped his shirt again. "Grace drew up the contract. We gave old man Thomas a cashier's check about an hour ago. Everybody's gone to the ranch to celebrate. I…" He looked up and across the rafters. "Just wanted to stop by a minute."

"Closing the deal on a Sunday?"

"Timing is everything." The guy was practically glowing from barely contained excitement.

Abbie didn't have to imagine what was running through Jamie's mind, she still remembered every blessed sensation that oozed through every pore the day she signed the papers for the café. The last thing she'd had in mind when she'd agreed to come to Tuckers Bluff was that one day she'd own the café in the little town that had saved her sanity.

"Don't look so lost." Jamie's smile shifted from one of delight to reassurance. "It will be fine."

For a small moment she thought he could read her mind before common sense kicked in and she realized he was talking about the two restaurants. Her response to folks since word of the new business had shifted from rumor to reality weeks ago had been the same. There'd be no liquor at the café, no dance floor at the café, and nothing needed to change. That was her story and she was sticking to it. And if she repeated it enough, maybe she'd eventually stop second-guessing herself. "I'm not worried."

"You don't look convinced."

"Maybe it's because I'm not." Had she said that out loud?

Jamie moved a step closer. "I did a lot of research. You might lose a customer or two now and again, but others will come to replace them. Folks who have had no reason to come to Tuckers Bluff will come now to dance or drink. Many of these people will prefer to eat first at someplace with a larger, more diverse menu. These will be customers who don't already live in town to patronize the café. It will be a good thing for both our businesses."

"You sound so sure." He really did. What was it about the

Farradays that they all held so much confidence? No matter what piece of garbage life threw at them. No matter how many Henry Wiggins and his ilk crossed their paths. They could hold a parade into hell and, waving a flag and cheering them on, everyone would follow.

"That's because I am. This isn't a whim. No one opens a restaurant in the near middle of nowhere if they haven't crunched the numbers. Especially not a big organization like Crocker."

"Yeah, well, that's great for you and Crocker, but that's probably what Walton told all the mom and pop shops in the *near middle of nowhere* when he opened his first box store."

Something very close to anger burned sharply in his gaze. "I'm not Wally. We're not on a mission to take over the world, or the town. O'Fearadaigh's will be good for both of us." The tone in his words softened. "Believe me."

What was it they said about the road to hell? "If you don't mind, I think I'll believe it when I see it." Not that she didn't trust Jamie or the Farradays, but if their luck were going to run out, she'd be first to bet it would be with something that her life depended on. After all, what were the odds a Farraday would save the day every time her world turned upside down?

• • • •

In the years since graduating school, Jamie hadn't spent nearly as much time in Tuckers Bluff as he had as a kid growing up. Nonetheless, he'd been here often enough to understand Abbie was as much a part of the fabric of this town as the sidewalk and the streets, Wally World could never replace Sisters, and Jamie would never try to replace the Silver Spurs Café. Somehow he had to find a way to reassure her. For both their peace of mind.

"Well I don't see Frank." She rocked back on her heels, scanning the empty rear of the store and called his name. When he didn't respond, she turned to face Jamie. "Who knows what he's gotten into. I'm going to head home and take advantage of what's left of my afternoon off. Tell Frank I'll see him tomorrow morning."

Jamie nodded. "Will do."

Not till she'd turned the corner onto the sidewalk and disappeared from view did he go looking for Frank. Halfway to the back door, a rustling sound loud enough to catch his ear had him scanning the area. The movement of a single empty feed sack atop a pile in a nearby corner told him the guilty noisemaker—if there was only one—would be there.

The real question was did he want to go after the rodent now, or wait for construction to drive the critters away? The more sensible thing to do would be to set out some rat traps. Or get a cat. But apparently today, sensible wasn't in his vocabulary. Holding a broom handle he inched closer.

He'd almost reached the stack of empty bags when the movement stopped. Tightening his grip on the broomstick, he stood as still as the sacks. Like a ridiculous game of chicken, each of them seemed to be waiting to see what the other did. Seconds ticked by before movement started again. A small lift on one side, a smacking sound nearby, and then what appeared to be an all-out wrestling match broke out underneath. The sack lifted, dropped, seemed to float in the air as something much larger than a single rat wiggled underneath. What was he about to get himself into?

For a new approach, he took a step back, held the broom from the bristle end and hooking it under the edge, braced himself to whisk the top sack away when a definitely non-rodent paw trapped the stick against the floor. *What the heck?*

Tipping his head sideways as though that would make it easier to see what was underneath the loose bags, and gripping his broomstick, Jamie took half a step forward and tugged lightly at the wooden handle. The paw released its hold and withdrew. Two seconds later two paws followed by a brown-tipped nose popped out from under the pile of empty sacks.

"Okay buddy." Jamie got down on his haunches and tapped his palm against the concrete floor. "Whoever you are, come on out."

Before he could fully brace himself, the fluffy body attached to the nose came barreling towards him. About twenty pounds of puppy energy ricocheted across his lap, up his chest, down his leg, around his back, and over again until finally flattening him and licking his cheek. Using both hands to grab hold of the pup and laughing, Jamie pushed him down to his lap and sat up, holding him steady. "Where did you come from?"

With the wag of his tail and a short woof, the puppy tried to push forward again.

"Oh, no you don't." Securing the animal under one arm Jamie pushed to his feet, scratching under the mutt's chin with his free hand. "Your owner must be around somewhere looking for you."

Returning to his original mission to find Frank, Jamie opted to check the storage area. Tired of wrestling a squirming puppy, he set his new friend down on the ground. "Frank, you in here?"

"Yeah. In the loft."

Loft? Jamie had checked the place out thoroughly and didn't remember anything about a loft.

Puppy let out a succession of three fast woofs then took off in the direction of Frank's voice and the pull down stairs at the back end of the former warehouse area.

"Hey buddy, wait for me."

Two booted legs came down from the ceiling, finding purchase at the top step. "I don't think anyone ever cleared out this area."

"I didn't even realize there was anything up there." Jamie moved closer to the stairs, the puppy dancing circles at the base.

"I'm not surprised. I almost didn't see it myself. More of an attic really, but I happened to notice the recessed pull and then I spotted the hook arm hanging on the wall over there." Frank took his time descending the rickety steps. "I thought it was just over the little office in the corner but it goes all the way to the back of the building. Same square footage as downstairs. There's furniture up there, crates, trunks. And judging from the period pieces, I'd guess a good bit of that stuff is over 100 years old."

Frank reached the second to last step at the exact moment Puppy barked and leaped upward onto the steps, bumping into Frank's boot.

"Whoa." Frank swung one leg outward to avoid stepping on the puppy. "For land sakes, where the hell did that thing come from?"

Wagging his tail and running circles around the foot of the ladder-like steps, Puppy barked up at Frank.

"Tell me we don't have another one." Frank released his hold on the ladder, taking the last step onto the ground just as Puppy did his dance routine underfoot bumping into Frank. Skidding under the steps, the bundle of fur in motion sent Frank tumbling to the ground.

"Buddy, no!" Jamie shouted, rushing to Frank's side. "Are you okay?"

Flat on his back, Frank blinked upward. "Define okay."

Jamie had to bite back a laugh. It had been a stupid question. Assuming being alive was a good thing, then he was okay. But judging by the way his foot twisted under the last step, Jamie did not need to be a doctor to know Frank was definitely *not* okay. "Don't move."

"Thought hadn't crossed my mind." Frank grit his teeth. "At least not until I can feel my leg."

Crap. This was *so* not good. Phone in hand, Jamison tapped speed dial for his cousin Brooks.

"You on your way yet?"

"Nope." Jamie looked at the puppy sitting perfectly still beside Frank. *Now he sits.* "Got a small problem here."

"How small?" All playfulness had slipped away from Brooks' tone.

"Frank fell from the pull down steps at the new restaurant. If his foot isn't broken it's awfully close."

"I'm more than halfway to the ranch but I'll turn around. Have you got him stabilized?"

"Does lying flat on his back count as stabilized?"

"Comedian. Any signs of injury other than his foot?"

Jamie held two fingers in front of Frank's face. "How many fingers do you see?"

Scratching the puppy with one hand, Frank looked at Jamie's hand waving in front of him. "Two."

"What year is it?"

"Oh, for the love of Pete. Stop playing Marcus Welby and just tell your brother to get his backside down here. I've got to get this foot taped up and ready for work before tomorrow morning."

"You hear that?" Jamie said into the phone.

"I'm pretty sure the whole county heard that. If you've got access to some ice, no harm in using it. And if he plans on going to work tomorrow morning, you'd better hope you're a lousy doctor and that foot isn't even close to broken."

Visions of Frank flipping burgers, wobbling on one foot, flashed through Jamie's mind like scenes from a really bad play. His gaze shifted to the foot still hooked at an awkward angle. If Abbie was upset that he and his family would be opening a dinner pub in town, when she learned he'd incapacitated her only cook, upset would be an understatement. He didn't have the slightest doubt. Abbie was about to kill him.

CHAPTER THREE

Pacing in the small waiting room, Jamie didn't know what was worse, the silent pained grimace on Frank's face as they moved him to Brooks' clinic, or Abbie's brave efforts to hide the worry and concern he clearly saw in her eyes.

"Well," Brooks came out from behind closed doors, "do you want the good news first, or the bad?"

"Good" and "bad" tumbled over each other as both he and Abbie responded.

The clinic front door burst open, Sister and Sissy scurrying in like hungry children late for supper. Tall and slender, Sissy spoke first. "We just heard. How is poor Frank?"

"I was about to explain--"

Aunt Eileen came barreling through the same doors, Uncle Sean only two steps behind her. "Got here as fast as we could once we heard Frank had fallen. How bad is it?"

The shorter of the two sisters turned to his aunt. "That's what we want to know too."

Jamie shifted around the growing crowd to move closer to his cousin. "I'm thinking we could all use a little good news."

"Good news? Then he's going to be just fine," Aunt Eileen interrupted.

"Eileen." Sean Farraday slid between his sister-in-law and the two mismatched owners of the town general store. "Give the man a chance."

Straightening her shoulders and jetting out her chin, Abbie ignored the chatter and looked to Brooks. "At this point I don't care if it's good or bad news, I just want to know how Frank is."

Brooks opened his mouth ready to speak, then paused to glance at the front door as though expecting someone else to fly in and interrupt.

“We’re it,” Aunt Eileen spoke. “Rest of the family is waiting at the ranch.”

“And we didn’t say a word to anyone else,” Sister said. “We ran straight over as soon as we bumped into Ned.”

Jamie didn’t want to know why Ned the mechanic, who was older than dirt, knew about Frank’s injury. All he wanted to know was what they were up against.

"His foot is not broken."

Jamie could actually feel the air shift with a group sigh of relief.

"But he might've been better off if he had,” Brooks continued.

Aunt Eileen frowned. "I don't like the sound of that."

"With a clean break we know we’re looking at a six week recovery. Frank’s got soft tissue damage."

"Torn ligaments?" Abbie asked.

Brooks nodded. "And tendons. To make things more difficult, he’s injured this ankle before."

"I don't remember him having a hurt leg." Sissy turned to her sibling. "Do you remember that, Sister?"

The shorter of the two, with a bee hive hairdo that would do any Texas matron from the nineteen fifties proud, shrugged. "For as long as he's lived in Tuckers Bluff, I've never known him to have a hurt foot."

"I don't think that it's possible for a man to make it through twenty years as a career Marine and get out without a bad something or other for a reminder of his service." Uncle Sean shook his head.

"That's right," Abbie hissed. "He's got a bad knee. I've always assumed it was from his days in the Marine Corps, but he's never confirmed that."

"He didn’t say,” Brooks continued. “Bottom line is he's looking at quite a few weeks before he's back to normal. Minimum one week no weight at all on that foot and then we can re-evaluate.”

Uncle Sean shook his head. "He is not going to like that."

The crease in Abbie's brow deepened and Jamie knew Frank wasn't the only one for who weeks off his feet was not a good thing.

"Frank is a man of few words." Brooks looked to his dad. "And the ones he shared when I told him I expected him to keep his foot elevated above his heart until the swelling was completely gone would get my mouth washed out with soap even at my age."

"Well," Aunt Eileen rubbed her hands together, "guess we'd better take him home."

The two sisters nodded. "He's going to need looking after."

"Exactly." Aunt Eileen looked to her nephew. "He'd best be coming home with us."

This time the two sisters shook their head. "No point taking him all the way out to the ranch. He can stay with us. Sister and I will look after him."

"What about the shop?" Uncle Sean asked.

Sister shrugged. "We can make that work. No need for both of us to be there all day."

"That's right," Sissy agreed, looking a little too satisfied for her own good. "This town looks after its own. Frank is one of ours."

The words almost made Jamie spit with laughter. He'd been visiting the ranch the year that Frank came to town. One of their own wasn't quite the words he'd remembered the sisters using at the time.

"Can I see him please?" Abbie asked, her voice low and strained.

"Of course. I gave him something for the pain. Not much. The man is stubborn, amongst other things. But he's expecting you."

Abbie nodded and moved slowly forward. He could only imagine all the things running through her head. He didn't know the history between Abbie and Frank, he didn't think anyone in town did, except maybe DJ. But it was no secret to anyone in town that Frank Carter would lay down his life for Abbie. Same as any man would for a sister, mother or daughter.

Increasing his gait to catch up with her, Jamie gently took hold of her elbow. "I'll come too, if that's okay."

Abbie merely nodded.

Eyes closed and his hands across his chest, Frank looked almost peaceful. Only the bandaged ankle nearly twice as thick as the other foot and propped up high on a pile of pillows gave a picture of reality. And right now, reality was one hell of a mess.

• • • •

There's been a small accident. From the moment Jamie uttered those words, Abbie's heart had not been able to slow to a normal rhythm. Not until Jamie explained only Frank's ankle had been hurt from falling down the pull down stairs had she been able to expel the breath she'd been holding.

Frank had saved her life in so many ways. From that fateful day nobody could ever forget, to the day he moved to Tuckers Bluff to cook for her café, and every day since. She couldn't imagine life in Tuckers Bluff without him.

Even now she worried. Could he have hit his head? Could there be more internal damage obscured by the attention to his foot? If he refuses meds, would blood clots be a problem?

Reeling in every rogue thought and concern by reminding herself what a fantastic doctor Brooks was, and knowing he cared as much about Frank, almost as much, as she did. "If you wanted a vacation, you could have just asked." She wished her voice hadn't come out quite so shaky.

The corner of Frank's mouth lifted into a snarl that substituted for a smile. "Vacations are overrated."

Stepping up beside the exam table, she laid her hands over his and squeezed. "Like it or not, it looks like you're gonna have one now."

Frank groaned and rolled his eyes. "Not happening. I'll be up and about tomorrow morning, same as always. You can count on that."

Her gaze shifted briefly from Frank to Brooks. The family physician remained silent and shook his head.

"I have it on good authority," Abbie patted his hand, "you are on mandatory rest. At least until the swelling is gone."

"Bull..." He paused. "Feathers."

If her world wasn't about to spin around on its axis, she might have laughed out loud at Frank's efforts not to curse in front of her. After all, it wasn't like she hadn't heard him use a few choice words before. Apparently living in the small Texas town for as many years as he had, had done some good to his vocabulary.

"Like it or not, you're staying off that foot until the doc says it's okay to be up and about."

"No offense, Doc," Frank waved a finger at Brooks, "but it will take more than just a twisted foot to keep me down. Good laced boot and I'll be ready to go."

Brooks chuckled. "Even if you are ornery enough to work on that ankle—against doctor's orders, mind you—you'd have to get past that bunch out there."

"What bunch?" Frank turned his attention to the closed door.

"It seems," Jamie spoke for the first time, "that you have an abundance of potential nurse maids."

Frank looked at Abbie. "What the hell is he talking about?"

"Common sense says you can't stay off your foot and take care of yourself at the same time," she explained.

"Says who?"

"My aunt," Jamie and Brooks echoed.

"And," Abbie added, "the sisters."

Letting out a deep groan, Frank dropped his head back on the table. Shaking his head, the scowl that had been permanently in place gave away to a soft chuckle that slowly grew into rumbling laughter.

Shaking off the nervous edge that regurgitated in her gut at his bizarre reaction, Abbie hefted one hand onto her hip. "And what may I ask is so funny?"

"Of all the times in my life, and there have been many, when I imagined what it would be like to have women fighting over whose bed I would sleep in," Frank waved a finger at the door, "not once did any of that lot come to mind."

The two Farradays quickly covered their mouths. Jamie suddenly found the floor very interesting and Brooks tinkered with the pen in his pocket. Both failing miserably to hide their laughter. Under any other circumstances, she might've found that comment funny too.

"You will be more comfortable with help," Brooks added.

Frank merely groaned.

"If you want to move into the apartment upstairs from the restaurant, then I can run up and check on you every little bit. Make sure you're eating and keeping your foot up."

"That's not half a bad idea," Frank agreed. "I can stay in the apartment upstairs, but you won't have time to run up and down stairs. I'll just come to work in the morning."

Brooks shook his head. "No work."

"She needs me," Frank grumbled.

"Says who?" Abbie barked back. Just because it was true didn't mean she had to let him know it.

Balancing on his elbows, Frank winced when the movement jostled his foot.

"And that," Brooks pointed, "is why you need to let your foot heal."

Frank shook his head at Abbie. "You can't work the kitchen *and* wait tables. Someone has to cook, and it isn't you."

"I'll do it."

All heads in the room turned to Jamie.

"Don't look so surprised. I do know my way around a kitchen. I'd have no business running my own pub if I didn't."

Surprise slid away from Abbie's gaze. She turned to face Frank. "There you have it. *He* can cook. Now, who's gonna take care of you? The Farradays or the sisters?"

CHAPTER FOUR

"Two pairs, Queens high." Eileen Callahan, aunt to the massive Farraday clan, looked over her shoulder at Abbie a few tables away. The poor thing was as jittery as the proverbial long-tailed cat in a room full of rockers. Eileen knew how the woman felt. This wasn't even her café and the thought of Abbie's livelihood depending on Eileen's nephew the bartender working in the kitchen, made her wish all she had to worry about were a few rocking chairs and an emergency trip to the vet. At least she could rest easy knowing that Frank was being well cared for at the ranch. Though the way Sister argued with Sean and later fawned over Frank when Brooks let them all in to see his patient, Eileen had a feeling that Sister might have been motivated by a little more than neighborly consideration. The way Frank quickly chose the ranch, he most likely had gotten the same impression.

Ruth Ann blew out a soft sigh. "Usually a pair of queens requires more than one but less than three."

Glancing at her cards, Eileen had no idea what happened to the other queen. "I know I had two."

Dorothy picked up a discarded playing card. "I think this is what you're looking for."

"Oh, of course. Simple mistake. I was distracted."

Sally May tossed her hand onto the pile in the middle of the table. "I know we're not playing for real money, but distraction is not an option."

"Except for her." Dorothy jerked a thumb in Ruth Ann's direction.

Ever since Ruth Ann had started dating Kelly's great uncle Ralph, from time to time she'd gotten increasingly more distracted in her card playing. Eileen guessed it was like the old cliché; lucky in cards, unlucky in love. Or in this case, lucky in love, unlucky in cards. Or would that be distracted in cards. *Whatever.*

The clamor of clashing metal rang out in the café and Abbie took off in a mad dash for the kitchen.

Shuffling the deck, Dorothy paused and leaned forward. "That's the third time this hour. Do you think maybe one of us should go see if we can help?"

Eileen bit her lower lip and shook her head. She'd wanted to jump up and run to the kitchen after the first time the crashing sound of metal ricocheted through the restaurant.

"So," Ruth Ann cut the deck, leaning in conspiratorially, "if we're not going to do anything to help, why in heaven's name did we show up for a special card playing session at the crack of dawn?"

Eileen sucked in a deep breath and reached for the first card dealt her way. The social club always started their card games early in the morning, but rarely were they the first customers in the door. "Moral support."

Sally May rolled her eyes and muttered, "Moral support my foot."

A full tray on her shoulder, Abbie came hurrying out of the kitchen and rushed past the card playing friends to the table behind them. To her credit, Abbie had plastered on a pleasant smile and took her time setting out the plates and dishes at the neighboring table, taking a moment to chat with the customers the same as she did on any ordinary day of the week.

Except for all the noises that didn't usually come from the kitchen, if Eileen weren't privy to what was actually happening today, she'd have no clue someone new was doing the cooking.

"It would help if Donna hadn't called in sick at the last minute." Sally May sorted her cards.

"It's not her fault her little girl has the flu. Besides, under normal circumstances with Frank in the kitchen, Abbie can handle this place with one hand tied behind her back."

"I suppose on the bright side," Ruth Ann rearranged her cards, "breakfast crowd is almost over."

A fresh set of cards in her hand, including two aces, and no surprising sounds from the kitchen, Eileen nodded and decided perhaps everyone's luck had changed.

"Anyone like their coffee freshened up?" Abbie held up a pot, her smile a little tired.

All the card players shook their heads. Even if they'd wanted another cup, no one dared to take up Abbie's time.

Eileen wasn't totally sure, but she thought she heard Abbie mumble "bless you" under her breath moments before the old-fashioned bell tinkled above the door announcing the entrance of a new customer. In almost choreographed precision, three voices across the table, including Abbie's, muttered "uh oh."

Eileen dared to glance over her shoulder. A parade of new customers pushed through the doorway. Tourists. From the way they continued to pour in, Eileen guessed one of the bigger buses.

Abbie's jaw almost hit the table. Her skin went ashen gray, and a rim of white surrounded surprised eyes.

Shoving back her chair and pushing to her feet, Eileen rested her hands flat on the table, leaned forward and whispered to her friends, "Now, girls. Now."

• • • •

Apparently working in a kitchen was almost like riding a bicycle. Slowly getting back his rhythm, Jamie had only dropped the hotel pans a few times. Of course, he'd never actually been a cook, but any restaurant manager would tell you that when an employee is a no-show, he learns fast how to cook, bus, prep, or wash dishes. Jamie had done his share of all of the above. Except right now he wished before moving on to barkeep, he'd done a lot more of the cooking and a lot less of the table busing. Had he not felt guilty as hell for Abbie's only cook being down for the count, he might have waited for someone more qualified to step up. Qualified or not, since the visiting pup who had actually caused the problem couldn't cook, and it was Jamie's future place of business where Frank had taken the dive, here Jamie was cooking in a strange kitchen. Praying not to screw things up too badly and extremely thankful Frank was as good at his job as everyone gave him credit for.

This morning, Jamie had anticipated cooking *a la minute* from scratch, meal by meal, searching for ingredients and fumbling his way through a foreign kitchen. It shouldn't have been a surprise to find Frank had left all the food prep for today ready before leaving yesterday. Jamie was even happier that the breakfast crowd was dwindling before his breakfast *mise*, the prepped items and ingredients for the morning dishes, ran out.

The double doors sprang open. Abbie hurried in, but rather than stop at the pass to leave an order, she rushed past him.

"What are you doing?" he asked.

Abbie grabbed an apron from a hook by the back door slid it over her head and wrapping the strings around, tied it tightly. "Tourist bus just pulled in. You're going to need help."

Before he could utter a word, Dorothy, one of his aunt's dearest friends and his cousin DJ's grandmother-in-law, pushed through the double doors.

Casting an observant glance from left to right, Dorothy nodded. "I've never been in here before. Not bad." Slapping her hands together she faced Abbie. "Which way are the aprons?"

Since Abbie stared at her with the same surprise he felt, Jamie supposed she hadn't expected company in the kitchen any more than he had.

"Eileen sent me in here," the older woman explained. "I've been assigned to do the meese. Whatever the heck that means. Which way?"

Blinking, Abbie nodded and pointed to the back door. "There's an extra apron over there. When it's tied on, follow me to the fridge."

Working as fast as he could in the unfamiliar kitchen, Jamie plated the next orders and slid them onto the pass for pick up. About to ring the bell, he realized the only waitress in the place was in the refrigerator with Dorothy.

The double door swung open again, and in marched his aunt. “We've got one heck of a crowd. Ruth Ann and Sally May set up three twelve-tops and two four-tops."

Great. Jamie took a deep breath. First day on the job and forty-four extra customers for breakfast. *Just peachy.*

"Four-top number one,” his aunt read from a pad in her hand. “That'll be two cowboys with spurs hold the onions on both. My guess is those folks plan on doing some kissing later in the day. I'll need two dots and a dash, and an Adam and Eve on a raft." Eileen spun about and called over her shoulder. "Don’t you worry none, Abbie. Sally May is already working on a fresh pot of coffee. Oops, dirty water."

Giggling as though this were the most fun she’d had since she was six years old, his aunt waltzed back into the cafe.

Stunned silent, he turned to see Abbie frozen in place, arms laden with peppers, and onions and other fresh vegetables, staring wide-eyed at the closed doors.

"Did you know she could do that?" he asked.

Abbie shook her head. "Do you understand what she ordered?"

"Yeah," he nodded, slowly turning back to the closed doors. "I just hope she does."

• • • •

"Take a load off." Adam Farraday pulled a chair out for Abbie.

One by one through the day almost every Farraday, except Catherine and Joanna who’d been left in charge of Frank, had found an excuse to stop in and check on Jamie. And by extension, Abbie. Some had popped in for only a moment or two, like Connor and Finn, who had used going to the feed store as an excuse to come into town. Not that they needed two hulking Farradays to pick up an order of horse pills. Of course, when word got out that the Tuckers Bluff Afternoon Ladies Social club was waiting tables, Abbie had the largest lunch crowd she'd had since that first day when Meg had shown up in town.

Now, at the end of the day, the only people left in the café after the dinner crowd were the three Farraday brothers who lived in town. Two with their wives.

Brooks waved a hand at the chair beside his brother. "I could make it doctor's orders. Sit."

Abbie knew the worst thing to do at the end of an insanely long day was to stop and sit, but she also knew there was no point in arguing with a Farraday, never mind three of them. She sank slowly into the wooden chair.

"Better." DJ smiled at her. "That's my girl."

Becky squeezed her husband's hand and sprang from her seat. "I'll go get Jamie. He probably needs a break too."

"How come you're not home with your wife and baby?" Abbie looked to Brooks.

Smiling as wide as Main Street, Brooks pushed to stand. "As a matter of fact, now that I can personally assure my wife that you are not frazzled to the bone or in need of medical attention, and cousin Jamie did not do anything to merit you killing him today—"

"That would be why I'm here." Laughing, DJ cut off his brother.

Brooks chuckled. "As I was saying, I can now go home and report to my wife that all is well, then call my sister to inform her that you will not be in need of her legal representation."

"Hardy har har." Jamie strolled to the table and spinning around the chair Brooks had just vacated, he straddled the seat, resting his forearms along the top. "Had I thought my life would be at risk, I would never have volunteered."

Meg sputtered with laughter. "I have a feeling General Custer may have said the same thing just before Little Big Horn."

The entire table, including Jamie, laughed along with Meg.

Jamie waved a finger at Brooks. "Before you go, who can tell me where the heck Aunt Eileen learned diner speak?"

"What?" several voices echoed.

Abbie bobbed her head. "He's not kidding. She marched into the kitchen this morning spouting coded breakfast orders as though she were on a reality restaurant TV show."

"Our Aunt Eileen?" Adam asked.

Jamie nodded and looked to Brooks, who shrugged, then to DJ who shook his head.

"All I know," Meg added, "is when I worked here at the café she never said a word to give any indication that she'd ever worked in a restaurant herself."

"Maybe that explains why she's such a good cook?" Becky asked.

DJ shrugged. "Well, it certainly could explain why she's so good at cooking for a lot of people."

"So, what we're all saying is that nobody has any idea where Aunt Eileen learned kitchen slang." Frowning, Jamie leaned forward. "Do we at least know what Aunt Eileen did before she moved to the ranch?"

All the Farraday siblings and in-laws looked around to each other.

"Didn't she sing or something?" Adam asked. Being the oldest when their mom passed, he was the most likely to remember anything mentioned around that time.

Brooks snapped his fingers. "That's right. She has a picture of herself standing in front of a microphone. I asked her about it once and she never really answered."

"Funny, I saw the same photo. It's in her dresser. For some reason I always assumed it was like karaoke night or something," DJ said. "If it were an important part of her life wouldn't it be *on* the dresser? Besides, who would walk away from a music career to take care of the lot of us?"

Even Abbie could answer that easily, and she wasn't a member of the family. Eileen Callahan. Today by itself was an excellent example of who their aunt was. On a dime, without a word having been spoken, she stepped in and pretty much took over the café for over three hours until Shannon came to work. And she roped all her friends into helping. Sure, Jamie was her nephew, and the whole town knew that Aunt Eileen was fierce about protecting her own. Today, Abbie might as well have been a Farraday.

She knew dang well this morning that any other card game day, and every last one of those women would've had their drinks refilled—often. But this morning they were more concerned with not making extra work for Abbie. Truthfully, she was a little surprised Aunt Eileen hadn't jumped in sooner. Every time Abbie had run to the kitchen after some horrendous crash, she discovered Jamie merely suffering the growing pains of working a new kitchen. Juggling and dropping a few pots and pans made for frightening noise in the restaurant and had every patron on alert, including Aunt Eileen, but she'd stayed put. Until the busload of tourists.

Abbie bit back a smile. That woman truly was amazing. Now, more than ever, like the rest of the Farradays, Abbie really wanted to know, what was Aunt Eileen's story?

CHAPTER FIVE

Standing on his feet was nothing new for Jamie. Bartenders stood for long shifts, but today had to be one of the longest days of his life. Not until he'd taken a seat beside his cousins had he realized just how bone tired he was. How Frank and Abbie did this, day after day, week after week, year after year, he didn't have a clue.

Across the room, Abbie locked the café doors. He knew she had to be as tired as he was, and yet she insisted on staying late to help him prep for tomorrow. All day he'd seen her come and go, in and out of the kitchen. A few times he'd had the luxury of pausing to watch as she fluttered about. The thought crossed his mind that perhaps this was how Frank made it through his days. Most of the time Abbie wore a smile that when flashed in his direction offered a jolt of energy to help push him through.

"All ready?" Her smile held in place, she yanked a toothy clip away from her head and shook out cascades of chestnut brown hair, then stretched her shoulders and neck before twisting her hair back into a bun, reattaching the clip, and heading for the double doors into the kitchen.

As the dinner crowd had wound down, he'd taken Frank's advice and began the prep work for tomorrow's menu specials.

"I know Frank plans his menu out at least a week in advance. The problem is, he doesn't actually write it down anywhere."

Jamie followed Abbie into the kitchen. "I know."

She turned to look at him over her shoulder. "You do?"

The phone in his pocket sounded, and he knew at this hour it could only be one person. Not bothering to look at the screen, he swiped at the phone. "I'm in the kitchen."

Frank's deep voice rumbled through the line. "How much did

you get done?"

"Quite a bit. You were right."

"Of course I was right. You think I was born yesterday?"

Jamie had never been in the military. He'd never had the pleasure of a drill sergeant dragging him out of bed before dawn and screaming in his ear about absolutely nothing before his first cup of coffee. Regardless, he was savvy enough to know not to respond to that particular question.

"I hear footsteps," Frank muttered. "That woman has bionic ears. I swear she can hear a cricket snore. I'm supposed to be resting. I'd better go. I'll keep the phone close if you have any questions."

"Got it. Go rest."

"Now you sound like your aunt. I hurt my foot, not my mouth."

His aunt's voice grew louder, but not close enough for Jamie to make out her words.

"I really gotta go. You take care of everything." The call disconnected.

Jamie had to laugh. How many people could have a former Marine drill sergeant backing down? Only one that he knew of. Force Eileen.

"That doesn't sound like the first time he's called." Abbie waved a finger at his phone.

Slipping the cell into his breast pocket, he nodded. "You probably don't want to know."

Abbie's eyes grew surprisingly round. "How many times has he called?"

Jamie shrugged. "He didn't want to see you run into any trouble."

"Whoever heard of a backseat cook?"

"Don't be too hard on him. He cares about you."

The sudden softness in her gaze had him questioning if perhaps the relationship between Abbie and Frank was something beyond employer and employee. Her attention shifted to the prep area in the small kitchen. "Oh, you have been busy."

He liked seeing the pleased grin on her face. "Frank shared his routine. In painfully precise detail."

"Oh brother, he's been calling you *all* day long, hasn't he?"

Jamie smothered a smile. "Yeah, pretty much."

"I'll ask him to stop."

"That won't be necessary." Jamie moved to the other side of the stainless steel table and stood beside her. "When things were really busy, I simply didn't answer the phone."

Abbie's eyes widened. "Oh, I bet that went over like a lead balloon."

“He would have done the same. He’s a big boy."

“Right now, I’m not so sure about that.” She smiled again and Jamie wondered how he’d never paid attention to such a heartwarming smile before.

Between the work he’d already done under Frank’s instruction and the extra hands helping, the work for the next day was prepped and stored in the fridge in almost no time at all.

“If you’d like to use the upstairs apartment, you’re welcome to it.”

Jamie shook his head.

“It’s a long haul to the ranch and dusk comes early.”

Didn’t he know that. Raised on a ranch, starting the day in the pitch of night was pretty normal. Of course, he hadn’t been working after dark the nights before. “Thanks for the offer. For now, I’m fine. If it gets to be too much, I’ll let you know.”

Abbie nodded. “Fair enough.”

Standing outside the café doors, Jamie waited for her to lock up. “I’ll give you a ride.”

“Not necessary.” She spun about to face him, clipping the keys onto her purse straps. “The walk helps me unwind.”

Which was what Frank had told him during one of his nine million calls today. When she had a lot on her mind, she’d walk to work. “Makes sense. I’ll walk with you.”

She stopped and stared up at him. Slowly her brows buckled

over the bridge of her nose. When a deep-set frown appeared, he knew they'd been busted. "Frank."

It wasn't a question, but he nodded anyhow.

"I swear," she grumbled then whirled around. "This isn't exactly a high crime neighborhood."

Slipping his hands into his pocket, he flashed a smile and shook his head.

"But you're going to walk me no matter what I say."

Again, not a question, but he nodded nonetheless. "Frank is bigger and stronger than you. I'm not going home and reporting that I let you walk home alone."

Hefting her purse over her shoulder, she rolled her eyes and shook her head, mumbling, "Men."

"It would," he waved to the lone car left in the side parking lot, "be a blessing to my tired feet if I could just drive you home."

Her gaze darted down the block then back to him. For a second he felt sure she was going to go all drill sergeant on him when her shoulders unexpectedly sank in rhythm to a deep exhale. "Fine. But Frank and I are going to have a nice little chat tomorrow and settle a few things."

"Better you than me."

Shaking her head and scowling, she turned away. Her steps heavier, she muttered something he couldn't quite make out but he was pretty sure the words *men* and *incorrigible* were in there somewhere and they didn't sound at all as playful as when she'd mumbled at him a few moments ago. Whatever was turning about in that pretty head right now didn't seem to show a very high opinion of the male species, and deep in his gut he had an unexpected urge to take on the task of changing her mind. How crazy an idea was that?

• • • •

How crazy was she to let a man give her a ride home—all four blocks of it. Though the true measure of her sanity should have been last night when she agreed to let Jamison Farraday cook for the café. Her soon to be competition. Competition that by the end of the week would have all of Frank's recipes. Maybe she should be asking how *stupid* was she.

"Whatever it is, I didn't do it."

Abbie blinked twice then dragged her gaze away from the window and focused on him. Maybe he was the crazy one. "Do what?"

"You were frowning and your back's as stiff as wooden plank. Whatever you're thinking, I didn't do it."

Just what she needed, an observant recipe thief.

Jamie pulled onto her street. "Which house?"

"Third from the corner on the right."

He pulled into the drive and leaning forward over the steering wheel, peered up at the house. "Cute."

"Thank you." She was darn proud of this place. Ten years ago she could barely make ends meet waiting tables in Dallas and here she was, owner of the café and her own little house. Before she could gather up her purse, and her energy, Jamie had circled the hood and stood holding the passenger door open. If anyone told her the Farraday men had the corner on the chivalry market, she'd believe them. "Thanks."

"My pleasure."

The door of his old truck slammed shut and Abbie spun around. "You don't have to walk me to the door." She stuck her hand out before he could speak. "Even Frank doesn't walk me to the door."

His gaze darted from her to the house, then to each of the neighbors' homes. She could almost hear the thoughts playing in his mind. Would Frank kill him if he stood by the truck? What if the boogieman is hiding behind the door? And if he's there, never mind Frank, his aunt and uncle would skin him alive. Kin or no kin.

"On second thought," she held up her hand, "why don't you come in for a cup of tea and you can tell Frank and your family there was no one hiding behind the shower curtain."

Jamie's eyes circled round as the full moon, the whites shining just as bright and Abbie had to laugh.

"Thank you, but if you don't mind, I'll just walk you to the door and take a rain check on the tea."

"Not going to check behind the shower curtain?"

He hesitated a beat too long and she knew he was actually considering it.

"Come on in," she laughed. "You can even check under the bed if you like."

Hands in his pocket, he walked heavily beside her. "You a mind reader too?"

"No." She stuck the key in the lock and ignored the little line forming between his brows at the number of deadbolts on her door. It had been a long time since she used them all, but knowing they were still there if she needed them helped her sleep more soundly.

Inside she flipped on the lights, tossed her keys on the nearby table, and spun around to face Jamie. "Last chance?"

Looking over her shoulder to the far end of her tiny house, he shook his head. "I think I can report back that all is well."

"Suit yourself." She stood slightly behind the open door.

For a half a second he paused as though reconsidering the checking under the bed thing, then moved forward. "See you tomorrow."

"Tomorrow," Abbie echoed.

Keeping his eye on the house, Jamie took a few steps backward along the walkway before turning toward his car.

The front door shut, she locked a single deadbolt. Maybe even back when she'd bought the place, three had been a bit excessive.

Anxious to get off her feet and crawl into bed, she resisted the urge to peek through the curtains and watch Jamie's truck roll away. Instead she stood, hand hooked around her neck, rolling her head and stretching until the last sounds of the rumbling engine dissipated into the night.

Tomorrow, when she wasn't brain dead after functioning all

day on only the few hours of interrupted sleep she'd gotten, she'd have to come up with a Plan B. For a crazy minute she wondered if Aunt Eileen could cook as well as she could wait tables.

CHAPTER SIX

"This shouldn't be so difficult." Sean set the whipped cream from dessert into the refrigerator and turning to face his sister-in-law, kicked the door shut with his foot. "The stubborn man is taking three steps forward and two steps back. That foot is going to take forever to heal at this rate."

"I swear that man makes an old mule seem reasonable." Aunt Eileen closed the door to the dishwasher and pushed the button.

Sean tipped his head in the direction of the bedroom hallway. "Anybody taking bets on whether or not he's in there right now strapping on a boot, planning his escape?"

"What are we going to do?" Eileen leaned against the counter. "He has a point. Jamie can't cook at the café forever. Soon he'll have his hands full working on the pub."

"True enough, but it hasn't even been a week. The ink on the bill of sale has barely had time to dry. There are a whole lot of new plans that have to be made before the first hammer gets picked up. That'll give Frank some decent healing time—if he'll cooperate."

Eileen knew Sean was right. Without the corporate backers and the family now making the decisions, there were already a few changes Jamie wanted to put back into the designs that Crocker had vetoed. Nothing major, but enough to require an architect to make adjustments delaying the start of demolition phase, and none of which was going to happen so soon that Frank had to push himself. "Okay, I know that, and you know that. Question is, how do we convince Frank?"

"I'd have better luck tying a bull's testicles with one hand."

She bit back a laugh. Why did everything that sounded so funny always have to hold a glimmer of truth? She wished just this once that Sean wouldn't have been spot on in his comparison, but dealing with an uncooperative pissed off bull would be a lot easier than dealing with Frank. As if proving her point, a crashing noise loud enough to be heard in the kitchen sounded too much like a raging bull trapped in a chute.

Tearing off down the hall, she arrived at the door in time to see Frank sprawled on the floor sans crutches. Stubborn didn't even begin to describe this thickheaded cook.

"Don't just stand there," Frank barked. "Crutches are next to the bed."

Sean shimmied around her and crossed the large bedroom in a few long strides. Holding the requested crutches in one hand, he outstretched the other to help Frank off the floor. "I know you're used to giving orders, but in this house it's customary to find a spot for the word please."

"Sorry 'bout that. Please and thank you." Balancing on one foot, he placed a crutch under each arm and swung himself the few steps to the bed then landed heavily on the mattress. "Don't know how those boys do it."

Eileen didn't understand — which boys doing what? Frank's expression was subdued, somber. He looked beaten.

"I forgot," Frank muttered, leaning the aluminum aids carefully against the wall. "Woke up out of a sound sleep needing to take a leak. Got up, took one lousy step on the good foot, then one with the other and landed hard on the floor like a felled tree."

Sean nodded and Eileen scrambled around to reposition an extra pillow under Frank's leg, wondering what she was missing.

"A few weeks and my life will be back to normal."

"If you follow Brooks' orders," Sean cut in.

Frank nodded and blew out a sigh, sinking more comfortably into the bed pillows. "I knew," he tapped his temple, "but I didn't understand." The same hand dropped to tap his chest.

There was no doubt in Eileen's mind that the pain in Frank's eyes had nothing to do with his injured foot.

"Too many of our boys are sent home with a new normal." Breathing out another sigh, Frank looked from Sean to Eileen. "In our minds we believe we understand what too many of them have gone through. Then standing up to find your leg won't hold you, well, this," he tapped his injured leg, "is true understanding. And let me tell you, it sucks. For those few minutes I might as well not have had a leg. I have no right to complain. From now on we'll do this the doc's way. Higher than my heart and no walking off into the sunset."

Sean didn't say a word for a long moment, merely dipped his chin in assent before glancing across the room and back. "Want some help to the bathroom?"

Frowning, Frank stared blankly at him. A moment later his expression more relaxed, he shook his head. "No. Guess I don't have to go after all."

"Very well. Think I'm going to call it an early night." Sean brushed passed his sister-in-law, giving her arm a gentle pat on his way out the door.

Tempted to fluff the pillows again, Eileen had spent enough years around men to know the gesture wouldn't be appreciated and retreated a step instead. Her mind wandered to a short time ago when Ethan had come home after the surgeries to save his leg. She hated that it was the thought of all the servicemen who'd lost limbs that subdued Frank into taking care of himself, but she hated even more that anyone had ever lost a limb at all. "If you need anything—"

"I know." Frank waved a hand at the bell on the nightstand. "Just ring."

"Rest well." At least now she wouldn't have to worry about Frank making things worse. Closing the bedroom door behind her, the sound of Sean in the kitchen surprised her. Standing by the sink, staring out the window, he'd set two mugs on the table and didn't flinch when the kettle began whistling.

Without saying a word, she turned off the gas, and kettle in hand, poured steaming water into the empty mugs.

Not till she set the kettle atop the stove again did Sean seem to notice she'd returned to the kitchen. "I meant to do that."

"I know." Eileen smiled up at the man she'd spent well over twenty years learning to read with the ease of the written page. "Want to tell me what's rolling around between your ears?"

Sean chuckled. That was the same thing she'd heard her sister ask him or the kids a thousand years ago. Tugging on his ear, he smiled at her. "Don't suppose I'll get away with immortality of the crab?"

"Nope." She poured sugar and milk into the tea and happily grinned at the use of her sister's other pat response. "Not this time."

Lumbering slowly to the seat in front of the hot tea, Sean took his place at the table. "We've been blessed."

Eileen nodded.

"We got all our boys back." He wrapped his hands around the warm mug.

She nodded again. "We did." Except for Brooks and Adam with years of post-graduate education under their belts, and Finn who was practically married to the ranch before he'd even hit puberty, all the Farraday men had spent at least some time serving their country. Of those who'd been deployed overseas, it was only Ethan they'd come close to losing. That they knew of.

"It's like Frank said. We know here," he tapped his temple with one finger as Frank had done, "but we can't possibly truly understand what it's like to lose a part of us until it's actually gone."

Thinking of Helen and how badly Sean had hurt for so long, she held in a sorrowful sigh. Not appreciating what you have until it's gone was a sad, honest truth. An image of the letter tucked deep in her dresser drawer reminded her some lessons could only be learned the hard way.

• • • •

After almost a week on the job as the café cook, Jamie had developed a healthier respect for restaurant staff. Unlike his cousins who had served time in the military, Jamie didn't fully appreciate the stamina of a former Marine until doing Frank's job all these days. It wasn't so much the job that was the challenge as much as doing it for 16 hours a day, all on his feet. From what Jamie could tell neither Abbie nor Frank took a lunch or dinner break.

Abbie pushed through the kitchen doors and standing in the threshold waived her thumb over her shoulder. "Adam and DJ just walked in looking rather dower. Chase is on his way too. As soon as you finish that last order, they've asked you to join them."

He didn't like the sound of that one bit. What would have his cousins and Grace's husband meeting grim-faced at the café? "Did they say something about Uncle Sean or Aunt Eileen?"

"No." Shaking her head, Abbie took another step inside, letting the doors slam shut behind her. "Something about the city council, which tells me it may have something to do—"

"With the pub," he finished for her.

Over the last few days, bit by bit, he'd been convincing Abbie that having two establishments in town could succeed. From the concerned look on her face over the future of his new venture, he hoped that meant he'd won her over to his way of thinking. The idea of losing the fragile foundation of his rather unconventional friendship with Abbie, and having it replaced with the cautious treatment of a rival, didn't sit well with him—at all.

She waited in front of the pass shelf for the two meals, and grabbing one in each hand, tipped her head toward the door. "Go on, hurry up."

Except for the young couple a few booths away from his cousins, and two tables of locals gabbing over coffee at the other end of the café, the place was pretty much empty in anticipation of closing time. Rather than slide into the booth, Jamie grabbed a seat and flipping it around, slid it over to the end of the table, straddling it so he could get up quickly if needed. "Tell me which one of you buffoon's wives locked you out of the house this morning?"

Like matching bookends, Adam and DJ's eyebrows shot up

high on their foreheads.

"Don't look at me that way. The only possible reason for such sour expressions is if your wives have kicked you out of bed."

Adam rolled his eyes and DJ leaned back blowing out a sigh.

“Another teen got his hands on some backwoods hooch and wound up in one of your offices?” Jamie teased.

“Lord no.” Adam shook his head. “Don’t wish that on anyone.”

“It’s not about our wives or a bad still,” DJ said quietly.

He didn't like the shiver running up his back. He’d been joking about the wives and the moonshine but maybe he’d been wrong and this wasn’t about the pub. "Something with the family?"

"Not the way you mean." DJ spotted Grace’s husband coming through the door and waved him toward the table. As soon as the in-law had settled into the booth, DJ leaned forward. "Why don't you fill Jamie and Adam in from the start with what you told me, then tell us all what more you have to report after the emergency council meeting."

“Emergency?” Adam muttered. “Has the city council ever done that before?”

DJ shook his head. “Not that I know of, which is why as soon as I heard it was going to be closed to the public, I knew we’d want to get some facts sooner than later.”

Chase nodded. "There are some perks to being married to the town’s legal counsel. She and the mayor are in a meeting still, but here’s what I’ve got so far. According to my wife, the only smart thing in the original contract between Crocker industries and old man Thompson was the no-fault kill clause. That allowed Jake to back out of the agreement at any time for any reason prior to the execution of final contract so long as he returned all earnest money received with the letter of intent."

"No one ever said old man Thomas was a fool." Adam looked to his brother-in-law. "Can we skip ahead a little bit and get to what’s going on now?"

Chase took a sip from the glass of water sitting at the table in front of him. "The point is that no matter how much Crocker grumbled about losing the building there was nothing legally they could do to come after Jamie or Thompson on that deal. Their hands were tied. Grace made sure everybody's backs were covered before we got involved insuring Crocker's annoyance would not be our problem."

"They were seriously not happy with me." Jamie smiled at the memory of Jeff Nimbus hollering on the phone. All is fair in love and war—and business. If Crocker could pull the rug out from under him they shouldn't have been so surprised that he'd be willing to do the same to them.

"What no one accounted for," Chase continued, "was Crocker not giving up on the idea of Hemingway's here in town."

"You're kidding me?" Jamie sputtered. "Where do they think they can put a restaurant of that size? The few available store fronts aren't large enough for an ice cream parlor, never mind a full-service restaurant."

"No," Chase shook his head. "Nothing available is an option."

A miserable thought crossed Jamie's mind. "Oh, don't tell me they're gunning for your place?"

Chase shook his head again. "They've requested a building permit."

"What?" several voices called out.

"You heard me. That's what the emergency meeting was all about. They apparently are offering some very lucrative incentives for fast action. They want to build at the end of town on land owned by Tuckers Bluff."

"Isn't that an interesting turn." Adam leaned back. "Jumping from one eating establishment to three."

"We can't support three," Jamie interjected. He'd done plenty of studies. Two restaurants were viable, three would do just enough damage to possibly put all of them under.

"Some of the council feels the same way."

"Good," Adam waved his hands. "Building permit denied.

Why are we here?"

"Because," Chase set his elbows on the table and leaned in, "some folks on the council only see dollar signs and others are on the fence because of the opportunity for more construction jobs."

"Temporary jobs," Jamie corrected. "O'Fearadaigh's would be doing the same with the renovations."

"That was Grace's argument, but it only got her so far. Remodeling and building from scratch are two different time tables."

Jamie didn't like the sound of that. "Spit it out."

"There was only one thing the council agreed on unanimously."

Everyone's backbone stiffened in anticipation.

"Within the town limits, only one liquor license will be issued."

"To who?" Adam asked.

"And that," Chase flattened his palms on the table, "is what they are meeting about now."

• • • •

There wasn't a single thing about the look on the Farraday men seated with Jamie that could put Abbie at ease. Brewing a fresh pot of coffee and getting a head start on filling the salt and pepper shakers were keeping her hands busy but not her mind. She really wanted to go eavesdrop, but if this was about the pub, then she had no business hovering. About to switch to filling the ketchup bottles, the overhead bell alerted her to new customers, a welcome distraction even this close to closing time.

Recognizing the two, she already knew what the orders would be. Same as always when teenagers came in. Two cheeseburgers hold the onions and a couple of colas. Caesar salad and diet drinks if they were girls.

Pushing the booth of Farradays out of her mind, Abbie smiled at the happy kids. "You boys are looking awfully chipper today."

The sandy haired teen she knew as the youngest of one of the larger ranching families beamed up at her. "Ordered a new hunting knife from Sisters. Just picked it up in time for our camping trip this weekend."

This wouldn't be the first or last kid to come through the cafe effervescing with delight over his new wilderness toy. In all the years she's lived in West Texas, Abbie still didn't understand the frontier fondness for knives and guns, but at least she wasn't afraid of them anymore. Truth was, if it came down to being trapped and helpless or having an armed Farraday or Brady, whether man or woman, young or old, she'd opt to have a ninety year old West Texas granny with a rifle any day.

Halfway to the kitchen, she spotted Jamie pushing to his feet and waved him back. With only these two kids and the few folks doing more chatting than eating at the other table, she had plenty of time to grill a couple of burgers.

Focusing on plating the order and not burning herself on the hot grill, Abbie had made it through without thinking even once about what was going on at the booth with Jamie and his family.

A plate in each hand, she could hear the excitement in the teens' voices. Heads together, they looked ready to conquer the world. "Here you go, boys."

Pulling apart and leaning back to allow room for the burgers, the kid with the new knife gripped it tightly in his hand, still yacking with his friend as though he held a butter knife and not a weapon that could gut an animal twice his size.

Sliding a plate in front of each kid, Abbie kept her gaze on the boys' faces as they lifted the buns and smothered the meat in ketchup. "Anything else?" she asked.

"Nope," one of the boys mumbled, grabbing his burger with both hands.

In a rapid movement, the other kid sliced his burger and, waving the ketchup covered hunting knife under her nose, turned to Abbie with a huge smile.

Any effort at avoiding the knife failed. Muffled words

sounded in her ears. The overhead light caught the glimmering metal and flashed in her eyes. More muted sounds hummed in her ears. The boy continued to wave the blade covered in red back and forth like a hypnotic metronome.

"Abbie." Loud and strong, her name penetrated the haze. "Is something wrong?"

Blinking, she lifted her gaze to the startled kid. "You okay, Miss Abbie?"

"Abbie." Lower, softer, her name sounded again. This time accompanied by a gentle grip on her arms. "Abbie?"

Jamie stood beside her looking as worried as the kid at the table.

"Put that thing away." DJ had followed Jamie to her side. Adam and Chase were a step or two behind. It took the kid a long moment to realize DJ meant his new knife.

Out of sight, out of mind. Sucking in a deep breath, she closed her eyes and searched for something to say. "Sorry, guys. It's been a long day."

The two teens shrugged. The kid with the knife held out his glass. "Could I have another drink, please?"

DJ stared at her, watching silently.

Jamie cast a quick glance to his cousins, first DJ, then Adam.

"One cola coming up." She spun about and spotted the Farraday men watching her the way they might keep an eye on a rattler about to strike. "I'm fine. Too much on my mind."

She turned away, quickly poured the kid a fresh drink, then hurried to the ladies room to regroup before everyone decided she'd lost her mind. Though for a few seconds there, maybe she had.

CHAPTER SEVEN

"Still no news?" Abbie reached for the BLT on whole wheat.

Jamie shook his head.

"I thought for sure you'd have heard something by now."

For the last two days he'd been on pins and needles waiting for more news from the town Council. The only thing they'd concluded the other night after meeting in private with Grace and the mayor was that they needed more time. He always considered himself a patient man, but right now time was not his friend and patience was fading fast. His family had invested a boatload of money in the building. A building that would be virtually useless if the town didn't issue them a liquor license. After all, what good was a pub that didn't serve beer at least?

"As a good friend of mine once said, don't look so lost. It will be fine."

Throwing his own words back at him actually made Jamie smile. Sundays were the only day the café closed early, and Jamie intended to use some of his free time to sort through the loft. He might not be able to start construction, but cleaning out the storage area was better than twiddling his thumbs.

A few more minutes and Abbie came back through the doors, setting a stack of dishes down. "This is it. Looks like were done for the day."

Jamie spied the clock over the doorway. "Closing early?"

"It happens. Once the Sunday afternoon slow down hits, that's it. Sunday is family day, and that's perfectly fine with me."

Family day. As far as Jamie knew, Abbie didn't have family in Tuckers Bluff. Thinking about it a minute, he realized he had no idea if she had family anywhere. Today completed the first full week working with her, and other than she had a lovely smile and an amazing work ethic, he knew little more about her now than he did seven days ago. "Got any plans for your afternoon?"

Abbie grinned from ear to ear. "A very hot date with a tall drink, the last ray of light, and a paint brush."

“Paint brush? Do you need help painting the house?”

That sweet smile that made him want to smile back bloomed. “Not that kind of paint. I like to paint pictures. Mostly oils, occasionally water colors but those are harder for me. I find it relaxing.”

He could certainly understand anything that gave her a chance to relax, but somehow it seemed wrong for her to spend her only day off alone. "I'm heading over to the building to start cleaning out the loft. Don't suppose you'd like to help?"

"Loft?"

"Well, it's more of an attic actually."

"Right. The place Frank had been snooping around before he fell."

Jamie winced. He’d sort of forgotten that part. "Sorry about that." He’d probably said that to her a dozen times a day for the first few days he worked here. "According to Frank there's some really cool stuff up there. Today will be the first chance I get to see for myself."

To his relief, her eyes twinkled with interest. "Frank did mention that he suspected some of the stuff up there could be well over 100 years old."

"I asked old man Thompson about it."

"And?"

"He groused that junk had been up there for as long as he'd run the feed store but didn't seem to know or care how it got there in the first place."

Abbie shook her head. "There's no understanding some people. I'm still amazed that old goat actually sold you the place."

"You and me both. When I found out how much more Crocker offered him to not kill the deal, I was flabbergasted that he turned them down cold."

"Well," Abbie shrugged, "I suppose deep down there's some good and loyal side to Jake Thompson."

Jamie smothered a smile. "Or he hates sushi."

Her brown eyes twinkling, Abbie laughed outright. "There is that."

"So, you curious?"

"Won't Aunt Eileen be upset that you're not at Sunday supper?"

Jamie shook his head. "Nope. Sunday supper is at Meg and Adam's later today. There's plenty of time to scour the attic."

"In that case, I think the Texas bluebonnets can wait a little longer."

"The what?"

"I like flowers." Abbie turned on her heel and pushed at the kitchen doors. "I'll be back to help you clean up in just a bit."

Flowers. He'd have to remember that. Something told him there weren't enough fresh blooms in her life. The door swung shut and Jamie took a minute to consider his temporary boss. The other night when she'd zoned out serving those kids hamburgers had been the first time he'd ever seen her anything less than totally in control. Even his first day on the job when she'd had to run in often to check on him, she never displayed any sign of frayed nerves. If DJ hadn't spoken with her privately and then assured Jamie that she was just fine, he might've shut the place down for the night whether she liked it or not. Had he seen even the slightest sign of something amiss the last couple of days he'd have pushed for more, but it was as though he'd imagined the whole thing.

Whatever was going on inside that pretty little head of hers, there was one thing he was definitely sure of. Abbie Kane was one helluva woman, and much like the attic in his old building, everything about her made him eager to uncover what more lay hidden behind her steadfast demeanor and wrinkle free uniform.

• • • •

"Good grief. You weren't kidding." Hands on her hips, as far back as Abbie could see the place was piled high with boxes and miscellaneous goods.

"I know there's a light here somewhere because Frank had it on the other day when we were talking." Jamie maneuvered around her, using the flashlight feature on his phone to find the light pull.

The old-fashioned chain made a familiar sound as Jamie yanked on it, brightening the crowded room.

"Wow." The place was a Mecca for antique enthusiasts. She could easily see Eastridge tables, Victorian settees, tables and chairs. Dark mahogany popular in the nineteenth century was everywhere. "Look at that."

Jamie chuckled. "Care to get a little more specific?"

"Those trunks." Lined along the left wall, Abbie counted at least two massive steamer trunks suitable for long ocean voyages and three or four smaller trunks. The kind people used nowadays for coffee tables or decoration. "I wonder if they're locked."

"I don't know, but hold on a minute." Jamie stepped to one side. "If you want to look at that first, we're going to have to make a path."

"No. Wait. Makes more sense to start here at the front and work our way back."

"That's a plan I can get on board with." He looked left then pointed to his right. "Why don't we begin in this corner over here? The boxes are cardboard and more recent than some of the others. Maybe it's just junk we can toss to make room for the other things."

Abbie nodded. "Works for me."

As predicted, the first box opened held outdated paperwork including fifty-year-old accounting ledgers from the Thompson feed store.

Flipping the pages, Abbie looked to Jamie. "How long did Thompson own this place?"

"I'm pretty sure he inherited the feed store from his dad. I have no idea how many generations before him ran it."

"At least one, according to this. Should we ask Chase if he wants them?"

"Good idea. I'll shoot him a text. We can set them aside for now."

The next few boxes were more paperwork. Some ledgers, some receipts, bills of sale and other notes. All for the Thompson Feed Store, and all old as dirt. Several open boxes were now stacked behind them when Jamie's cell phone beeped.

Taking a few seconds to read the text, he slipped the phone back into his pocket. "Chase said to pull out a few samples for nostalgia, but we can recycle or donate what's left."

Abbie scanned the neat pile of old boxes. “Do you think the library would like some of these records?"

“No idea, but I vote to take these boxes over another day and let Miss Marion decide."

Pushing to her feet, Abbie chuckled softly. "I still can't believe Tuckers Bluff actually has a librarian named Marion." She leaned over to pick up one of the boxes.

Jamie moved beside her. "What do you think you're doing?"

"Taking these downstairs to get them out of our way."

"Oh no you don't."

“What do you mean no?"

"I mean, I already lost you one cook, I am not losing your head waitress too. I'll take the boxes downstairs."

Abbie hugged the box closer to her. "And what if I lose you, then I’ll be out a cook again."

Hands on the box Abbie refused to let go of, Jamie frowned at her. "It looks like we have a stalemate."

Without releasing her grip, she shifted her weight. "So what do you suggest?"

"I suppose we could just toss the boxes down the stairs."

Abbie rolled her eyes. "Great. Then we can have twice as much of a mess to clean up."

"Okay. What if we line all the boxes along the edge of the

stairway, I go down with the first box, then you can meet me halfway and pass the rest off?"

She realized quickly what he wanted was to be at the bottom of the stairs to either catch her or break her fall. Such a Farraday thing to do. Chivalry was alive and well in West Texas and downright overflowing among the Farradays. "Deal."

With almost a dozen boxes sorted and out of the way, they had more room to reposition and organize.

"Looks like that's the last of the cardboard boxes. These over here are wood." Jamie pointed to some smaller crates. "There's a crowbar downstairs. I'll be right back."

Abbie nodded and worked her way around the front crates to the first trunk within reach. Delighted to find it unlocked, she blew some dust off the top and lifted the lid. "Oh my."

Crowbar in hand, Jamie climbed off the last step. "What did you find?"

“A little of this, a little of that." Gently sifting through the contents, she decided this had been someone's family trunk. Keepsakes of a lifetime. Hand crocheted baby booties. Infant christening gown. Handmade quilt. Perhaps a favorite party dress. A hand carved train engine worn right about where a playful little boy’s hands would have held the toy fascinated her. "Do you think these belonged to the Thompson family?"

Jamie squatted beside her. "I doubt old Jake would know. And I hate to say it, but I don't think he’d care either." He fingered the christening gown she laid neatly across the top.

“You like babies?” She hadn’t expected him to look so…interested.

A small hand carved rattle to one side caught his eye. “Doesn’t everyone?”

“Not really.”

Eyes wide with surprise met hers. “You don’t like babies?”

“I love them. Just saying not everyone does.”

“No,” he leaned back. “We wouldn’t need protective services if they did.”

Abbie studied him a long moment, wondering if watching all his cousins and siblings married and many starting families was making him feel left behind. “Penny for your thoughts.”

“If the town council smartens up and the pub becomes a reality, Tuckers Bluff is a good place to raise a family.”

“I think so.”

“You ever picture yourself with a family? Kids?”

“Not for a long time.”

“Why not?” His brows buckled with concern.

Abbie shrugged. For a split second she considered truthfully answering the question, but she couldn’t bring herself to share the fears that had once ruled her life for too long. Gently closing the lid, she turned her attention to the crates a few feet away. "We’ve still got a lot to do here. Might as well go back to opening the ones closest to the front."

An uncomfortable long moment passed as Jamie studied her too intently before nodding. With little effort, he was able to pop the lid off the first wooden container and removed the top layer of straw packing.

"Ooh," Abbie squealed. "Pictures.”

Jamie stood over her shoulder as she dusted off photograph after framed photograph, handing them to him.

“Hey, isn't this Adam's clinic?" Abbie held up a frame for Jamie to see.

"Yep. Back when it was a homestead. I'll have to give this one to Adam. I'm sure he'll want to hang it in his office."

"Or maybe the waiting room so the whole town can enjoy it."

Jamie nodded.

"And here's the feed store.” She handed it off to Jamie.

“Looks like this place had been in the family for a lot longer than old Jake thought.” Jamie held the picture of an older man in front of the Thompson Feed Store, a younger version of himself at one side, and a small boy at the other.

“Maybe Chase would like it?”

“I’m sure he would.” Jamie set the picture in the box of

paperwork for Chase.

Reaching the bottom of the crate, Abbie lifted two of the last framed pictures. “Oh my.”

“What?” Jamie leaned over.

“I didn’t realize colored photography was available so long ago. Someone was one hell of a photographer.” She held up one of the pictures. “This must be the Grand Canyon. Look at all those colors. Even faded, it’s like a velvet blanket of yellow and blue.”

“Actually,” he reached for the photo, “I think this is Big Bend.”

“You’ve been?”

He nodded and handed her back the picture. “Amazing place.”

“This would make a beautiful painting.”

“Would you like it?”

“Would I?” She glanced up from the frame in her hand to see him grinning at her. “What?”

“Your whole face lights up a room when you’re really happy.”

She could feel the heat reaching her cheeks. “These are lovely. Thank you.”

“So are you.”

Time and space seemed to come to a silent halt. Abbie had noticed long ago that Jamie had the captivating Farraday smile and twinkling light eyes, but not till this very second had she felt the heat of his gaze as strongly as though someone had wrapped her in an electric blanket. She didn't dare so much as blink an eye for fear of losing the connection. Unable to think, she couldn’t begin to guess just how long had it been since she had felt so perfectly warm and safe. Safe with another Farraday, only this one made her feel warm and fussy in ways the other Farradays never had, and didn’t that spell Trouble with a capital T.

• • • •

Though mostly working in silence, Jamie didn't want his time alone with Abbie—well alone with her and over a hundred years of ghosts and history—to end. Even if it meant being surrounded by a house full of relatives, he had only one possible idea to keep today from ending early. "It's almost time to head to Adam and Meg's for supper."

"Oh my." Abbie glanced at her wrist. One of the few people Jamie knew of who still wore a watch. "I didn't realize we'd been up here so long."

"And we've barely made a dent." He hadn't anticipated what a chore going back in time would be.

Straightening her back, Abbie slowly scanned the still untouched items in the long forgotten storage area. "I'd like to come back."

Just the words he'd wanted to hear. "I'd like the help."

The corners of her mouth lifted in a soft smile before she scooted across the dirty floor to fumble with the lock of another trunk. "Last one before you have to leave."

"About that." He shifted to sit beside her. "Thought you could join us for dinner."

"Oh, I look as worn out and dirty as some of these pieces."

"Ditto, but Aunt Eileen won't care. No one will." He brushed her hand already fidgeting with the lock of another trunk. "Please."

She hesitated just long enough for him to hope she'd give in, but fear she'd stand firm in her refusal. When she bobbed her head in agreement he let go of her hand and stopped himself before lifting his in a winning fist pump.

Already engrossed in the challenging lock, Abbie missed his near fumble. "This one seems to be stuck."

"Let me try." He reached around her and pushing at the ornate clasps, shoved them apart. "Dang it." Yanking his hand away, he quickly shoved his thumb into his mouth.

Frowning, she glanced in his direction. "You cut yourself?"

Nodding, he eased his thumb away from his mouth, swiped at the red droplets and pinched his thumb.

On her knees reaching for his hand, she hesitated midway between them and then shifted back onto her haunches. "We should have Brooks take a look at that."

"It's just a prick." Jamie lifted his gaze from his thumb to Abbie, surprised to see the hint of panic in her eyes. Nothing like the other night, but nothing he was used to seeing. "Hey, it's no worse than a paper cut."

"Yes." Abbie nodded, slow to shift her gaze away from his thumb and back to the trunk. "But still."

"Look at me." He waited a long beat for her gaze to meet his. Studying her blank expression, he considered the woman he'd worked with all week and the one he'd encountered a few nights ago. Something was very wrong. "Want to tell me what this is all about?"

She blinked a few times. "The latches are old and rusty. You might need a tetanus shot."

"Had one." He brushed the back of his knuckle along her cool cheek and softened his tone. "Want to tell me what's really going through your mind?"

CHAPTER EIGHT

Willing her mouth to find the words, Abbie squeezed her eyes shut and blew out a deep sigh. For the second time tonight, and the first in forever, she *wanted* to talk about that night. "It's a long story."

"I'm not going anywhere." Jamie remained calm and still beside her.

"What about Sunday supper?" She knew she was stalling. A part of her wanted to hop up and scurry away, but another bigger, deeper part very much wanted to tell Jamie how jumpy she'd been since that ridiculous knife had sliced through the ketchup covered piece of meat. More than anything she was angry with herself for letting something so ridiculous set her back so unexpectedly.

"Guess I'm not very hungry." His voice dropped, soothing her like a sip of aged whiskey. "Tell me."

"Don't know where to start." She sucked in another deep breath.

Jamie smiled at her. "What's your favorite color?"

"Purple." She forced a smile back at him. "Yours?"

"What kind of an Irishman what I be if my favorite color weren't Kelly green?"

Her smile came more easily this time. Her own fingers pressing into her palms uncurled. "Is it?"

Jamie nodded. "Though sky-blue comes in a close second."

"I like blue too."

"Favorite food?"

"Easy." Her shoulders relaxed. "Lobster. Less than a pound. With lots and lots of butter."

"Ah, I detect somebody perhaps has a New England background?"

She tapped the tip of her nose. "Dad was from New Hampshire. Every so often we'd go visit. Grandma always made us lobster the day we arrived. It was my favorite part of the trip."

"Beach or mountains?"

"Not so fast." She slid her legs out from under her. "Your favorite food?"

Jamie chuckled. "Oh come on. The way to a man's heart is through his stomach. Everything is my favorite food."

"None of that." Abbie shook her finger at him. "There has to be one special thing."

Tilting his head back Jamie studied the cobweb-covered rafters as though an answer were stitched alongside one. Dropping his gaze to meet hers, he held out his arm, extending his pinky. "Promise never to tell my mother or my Aunt Eileen?"

She linked her pinky with his. "Promise."

"I used to date a gal who came from an Italian family. Every once in a while she'd make meat sauce from scratch. It took all day. It was out of this world, but when she used it to make her lasagna. Oh. Heaven."

"Grams lived in New Hampshire but she hailed from an Italian neighborhood in Boston." Fingers still entwined, she flashed a toothy grin. "I'll bet Grams' recipe against your ex's sauce."

He shook his head. "Easy pickings. I've had Frank's lasagna."

"That's nice," she shrugged, pulling her hand away, "but Frank doesn't have Grams' recipe."

"Ooh," he sucked in a breath through his teeth, "a super-secret sauce recipe. You're on." Leaning back against a crate he shot her another question. "How long have you known Frank?"

"Since my first day waiting tables in Dallas. Everyone warned me to steer clear of the gruff former Marine. He barked orders at everybody as though they were his recruits. Bad ones."

"But he didn't fool you?"

Abbie shook her head. "No matter how hard he yelled, I could always see the twinkle in his eyes. Except once."

Jamie straightened. "The reason you froze when the kid wielded his knife the other night."

"It wasn't the knife alone that threw me off. I've seen plenty of knives. Frank uses huge ones to butcher beef. No, this was the perfect storm. That particular type of hunting knife, the ketchup, the juice from the burger, even combined I still could have held it together, but when he waved the dripping knife under my chin while talking." The fingers of her left hand dragged her shirt collar away from her neck, exposing a thin white line, then she leaned forward clasping her hands together in front of her. "That's when it all came flooding back."

Jamie's strong hand covered hers. "What happened?"

Already she'd told Jamie more than she would have any other person. She knew if she chose to stand up and walk away, he wouldn't ask again. But she didn't want to walk away. She wanted him to understand the part of her life that changed her world and tried to steal her soul. "After I'd been at the restaurant a few years, a new girl came to work with us. Nice. Sweet. Natalie went to college during the day and worked the dinner shift with us. I'd only met her boyfriend once, but something about him just rubbed me the wrong way. Reminded me of a snake oil salesman. Lots of charm and smiles but vermin underneath. Anyhow, his behavior shifted, became more controlling of where she went, what she did, trying to separate her from her friends, but she was smart enough not to fall for it."

Jamie's thumb began swirling motions across her wrist, giving her something comforting to focus on as she spoke.

"When Natalie broke it off," she continued, "he kept at it. Calling her at all hours of the day and night, showing up on her doorstep. Badmouthing her to her neighbors and anyone who would listen to him. The police couldn't do anything about it until he made the mistake of hitting her in front of witnesses."

"Restraining order?" Jamie asked

Abbie nodded. "For all the good it did us. Everything came to a head on a Sunday night. Natalie and I were the only two waitresses left. Frank was the main cook. A couple of other guys, kids actually, were working the kitchen with him. Manager was in the office. We didn't bother to lock the doors until the last customer had left."

She could feel the tension in Jamie's hand tightening to match her own.

"It all happened so fast. One minute we were cleaning up and the next Henry Wiggins stood in front of us waving a gun. It was crazy. He fired into the ceiling to get everyone's attention. Carolyn, my manager, came running out from the office, her cell phone in her hand. He whirled the gun at her and fired. I swear my heart literally stopped. She must've seen it coming because she ducked left behind the salad bar. I didn't know it at the time but she'd dialed 911 as soon as she'd heard the shots so the police were listening to everything.

"In the kitchen, Frank realized right away what was happening. Doesn't take much for a Marine to recognize the sound of gun shots and take action. I don't know that he knew it was Natalie's ex, but he knew we were in trouble and managed to get the entire kitchen staff out the back door."

"He stayed."

It wasn't really a question, but she nodded anyhow. "Henry fired another shot at one of the tables, sending the glassware flying. He was so focused on scaring Natalie and me that he hadn't realized Frank was in the building until he crawled out to bandage a woman's arm that had been cut badly by the shards of shattered glass."

She took in a calming breath and Jamie squeezed her hand. So engrossed in living the story, she didn't notice when he had laced his fingers with hers.

"By now there was a first officer at the scene." A nervous smile tugged at one side of her mouth. "DJ. Though I had no idea who he was at the time. He developed a rapid rapport with this character. When the hostage negotiator arrived, Henry would only keep talking to DJ. Your cousin did pretty good with him, considering the guy was truly certifiable. One minute he'd be sweet talking Natalie and the hostages, promising he wouldn't hurt anyone, that he just wanted Natalie to give him a chance to make her happy, and the next he was Dr. Jekyll firing the gun, making threats, accusing Natalie of cheating on him. Then DJ would talk to him and calm him down all over again. Talk about an emotional roller coaster. At some point DJ asked if he was hungry, and Henry screamed *I'm not eating any of your poisoned food*. Frank spoke up, offered to cook him anything he wanted, said he could watch and make sure it was safe to eat. Frank even offered to eat it first. Apparently, food, like music, can calm the savage beast."

Jamie inched closer, closing the remaining gap between them.

"For a brief few minutes, we thought DJ had finally convinced him to let us all go, but something inside snapped again. The bullet hit Frank. Natalie screamed, and when she tried to run to help, Henry grabbed her by the hair and told her she was his. Said that he was the only person she needed to worry about taking care of. Frank shook his head at us, waving his good arm, letting us know it wasn't serious. Anger fueled by adrenaline, Natalie pulled away and screamed at Henry that over her dead body would they be together."

Jamie winced, sucking in a short breath.

"Yeah. That's when he pointed the gun right at her and pulled the trigger. I couldn't possibly have stopped him, but I didn't have to. Nothing happened. I'd lost count of how many times he'd fired. He might've run out of bullets. It might've been a misfire. To this day I don't know how, but wounded and all, Frank lunged in Henry's direction. Like an idiot, I ran right in front of Henry to reach Natalie. Before Frank could get within grabbing distance Henry had pulled me against him, squeezing the air from my lungs with one arm. The other hand held the hunting knife against my neck. I'd been so focused on the gun, I hadn't even noticed the knife before."

"Oh, Abbie," Jamie whispered softly.

"Natalie jumped up, begging him to drop the knife. Pleading, agreeing to do anything he wanted. He seemed to get tremendous pleasure out of watching her grovel. I didn't even feel when he tipped the knife against my skin."

Mindlessly, she lifted her hand, one finger traced the tiny scar before falling back in front of her.

"Natalie was on the ground on all fours, promising the idiot anything he wanted. Frank was holding his wounded arm, promising Henry would live to regret the day he was born if anything happened to me or Natalie. And then DJ's voice broke through the haze. The same steady calm voice that had dealt all night with that lunatic. Easy and reassuring. Doing his job. Henry shifted his weight, turning his attention to the front door, loosened his grip. Next thing I knew gunfire ricocheted in the room and Henry's arm fell away from me. I was covered in blood. His blood."

"I'm sorry."

Blinking, Abbie lifted her gaze to meet Jamie's. "I was an emotional wreck for a long time. I tried to go back to work, but I couldn't do it. Eventually I thought to hell with the get back on the horse after a fall theory and went to work for a different restaurant. That didn't matter, every time someone came up on me unexpectedly, or the cook held a cleaver in front of me, or a car backfired, I'd jump. DJ had kept tabs on me, did his best to keep me grounded. We'd have coffee every so often until he left the force and moved home. Right about then was when I gave up working nights and took a job at a pancake house during the breakfast shift. Then one day a man came in who looked so much like Henry I actually questioned if I'd really seen him killed. DJ talked me off that ledge."

“Remind me to thank my cousin.” Jamie squeezed her hand. "What happened to Natalie?"

"She finished out the semester, packed her bag, and moved home to Nebraska."

"And you decided she had the right idea?"

"Not until the day DJ called and told me there was a waitress opening at the café here in Tuckers Bluff. I don't remember saying yes. I don't remember packing. I barely remember driving to West Texas, but as soon as I pulled into the parking lot I could breathe again. By the time the café owner showed me the room upstairs to use until I settled in, for the first time in a long time, I knew everything would be okay."

"And Frank?"

"Unlike me, the former owner was the cook. When she decided it was time to retire and moved to Florida, she told me she was putting the cafe up for sale. I had a little bit of money saved, not much, but I made an offer asking her to carry the balance until I could prove to a bank that I could make a go of it. There weren't a whole lot of people banging the door down to run a café in small town Texas. She agreed, I called Frank, and the rest, as they say, is history."

"And the kid with the knife brought it all back."

Abbie nodded. The only person she ever talked about that day with was DJ. Not even Frank dared bring the subject up. For years now the whole thing seemed truly behind her. Except for the day Meg was taken hostage at the hardware store, Abbie never really thought about it.

Sidled up beside her on the floor, Jamie draped an arm around her and whispered softly in her ear, "Is this okay?"

Nestling her head into his shoulder she nodded. "Very."

"I'm thinking we could stay here the rest of the night going through the boxes, or just sitting here like this on the floor…"

"I can just hear how that story's going to get retold around town like wildfire."

He placed one gentle finger against her lips. "Or we can go have dinner at Adam's, fill up with good food and maybe indulge in one of Toni's decadent desserts. The choice is yours."

"I do love her cake balls." Not waiting for her to think it through, her stomach growled, making the final decision. "I guess were going to Sunday dinner."

Despite feeling a little shaky, Abbie couldn't think of any

place safer then at Jamie's side, except maybe a Farraday kitchen.

• • • •

Nothing in his lifetime could have prepared Jamie for what Abbie had just told him. Crazy events like that are the sort of thing that happen to other people. People on the news. Not people you care about. And he did care. More than he probably should. If his cousin hadn't killed the low life years ago, Jamie for the first time in his life could easily see himself hunting that devil down and taking him out like the rabid animal he was.

The entire short ride to Meg's B&B, Jamie couldn't get the story Abbie had too aptly unfolded out of his mind. Not even the savory smells of a delicious dinner that smacked him in the face as he and Abbie crossed the threshold could snap his thoughts fully back to the here and now, and yet, Abbie had moved on. Made a better world for herself. Yeah, he'd been right all along, she was indeed one hell of a woman.

"Don't you look cozy?" Abbie bit back a smile. Tucked under a blanket on the big leather sofa, a book in his hands and cushions propping him and his foot up, Frank reminded him of a cattle baron of yesteryear recovering from some ranching accident.

Flipping the paperback closed, he mouthed, "Hardy har har."

"I'm with her." Holding a small box in one arm, Jamie pointed his other thumb at Abbie. "Is everyone in the kitchen?"

"Your aunt and some of the ladies have been in there laughing and cooking since church. I think DJ and Brooks are the only two missing." Frank tossed the book onto the nearby coffee table. "How are things going for you at the café?"

"Great." Jamie offered as much of a smile as he could muster after hearing what they'd both been through.

Narrowing his eyes, Frank studied him a moment. "Would you tell me if it weren't?"

"Of course he would," Abbie answered, "but he won't have to because he's keeping the customers very happy."

"Hmmph," Frank grumbled and reached for the book again. "Happy, my good foot."

Jamie smothered a smile. "I'm going to put this in the kitchen and let folks know we're here."

"I should clean up a little first." Abbie brushed her hands together. More than once since leaving the dusty former feed store she'd done the same, but probably still felt as dirty as he did.

"I was thinking the same thing once we checked in. Let me ask Meg which bathrooms we can use."

Abbie nodded, then turned to Frank. Poor guy had hoped to be back and on his feet by now, but after a week Brooks had handed down the sentence of another seven days without putting any weight on it. "Need anything from the kitchen?"

The man looked over the rim of his book to the stack of word puzzle books and empty dishes and glasses cluttering the coffee table then skewered her with an are-you-kidding-me glare.

"Guess not," she chuckled. "Whistle if you change your mind."

He harrumphed and again buried his nose in the paperback.

Scanning the old kitchen for Meg, Jamie dropped the box on an empty corner of counter space and continued around the island to kiss his aunt on the cheek.

"Oh, good." His aunt smiled up from the basket of warm rolls in front of her. "We were getting ready to send a search party out for y'all."

"You should see all the things stored in that place." Jamie reached for a bun and Aunt Eileen playfully swatted his hand.

"Don't spoil your appetite."

"No, ma'am." He uttered the only acceptable response since he'd learned how to talk.

"So glad you're joining us, Abbie." Aunt Eileen smiled. "I was hoping Jameson would invite you."

Across the room, Toni slid a tray into the oven. "You two look like you've been digging through a coal mine."

"Agreed." Jamie turned to Meg. "Is there someplace we can

wash up?"

"Sure. Head up to our apartment." Meg inched closer, waving at the dusty box. "Did you at least find something fun?"

"Actually," Jamie turned and pulled out a few of the pictures they'd found, "yes."

Wiping her hands on a dish rag, Meg came around to one side of him and Toni to the other.

Meg whistled. "Cool."

"What?" Grace peeked over Meg's shoulder.

Coming in from the back porch, Adam stopped at his wife's side and peered down at the photos now laid out on the island. "That's the clinic."

"According to the date on the back," Meg said, "about 150 years ago."

"Wow." Adam held the framed photograph and looked to his cousin. "You got plans for this?"

Jamie shook his head. "It's all yours. Old Man Thompson doesn't have any interest in the stuff in storage."

"Well," Aunt Eileen handed a stack of plates to Adam, "that doesn't surprise me at all. That old man only cares about his horses."

"Mostly his horses." Finn closed the kitchen door behind him. "He did give up a lot for his son when push came to shove."

"He has a point," Jamie added. "Could have something to do with why he was willing to sell the building after all these years."

Aunt Eileen handed another stack of dishes to Finn. "Maybe, but I'm not gonna waste my time trying to figure it out. You two," she waved a finger at Jamie and Abbie, "go on if you want to clean up. Dinner will be on the table shortly."

"Yes ma'am." Five minutes in the kitchen with his family and Jamie was at peace again. This was one of the biggest reasons he'd pushed for a pub in Tuckers Bluff. His gaze shifted to Abbie, hair down and swaying with her hips as she made her way down the hall and upstairs. Now he had two reasons for wanting very much to stay in Tuckers Bluff.

CHAPTER NINE

By the time Jamie and Abbie returned to the kitchen, all the food was set out on the massive island. Half the family had already taken their places around the dining room table.

Keeping a close eye on Abbie, Jamie noticed she'd hardly put any food on her plate. "We won't run out. If we did, it would be a first."

Scooping a little extra mashed potato onto the plate, she smiled up at him. "Saving room for dessert. That was a tray of cake balls Toni put in the oven."

"Smart woman." At least he hoped it was all about the dessert and nothing about reliving a nightmare.

"Would you two get the lead out," Grace called from the other room. "I'm hungry and we have a lot to talk about."

Holding the chair for Abbie, Jamie found himself wishing he could do so much more for her. Everyone finally seated, his cousin Finn did the abridged version of saying grace. The fact that neither his aunt nor uncle scolded his cousin for skipping from "thank you father" to "through the lips and past the gums" only showed how hungry everyone was. Or anxious to hear what Grace had to say.

Eileen split open one of Toni's homemade buns. "How did this simple idea get so crazy?"

"It should be an easy choice for the council." Jamie stabbed at his dinner. "A no brainer."

Grace nodded. "Remember, cousin dear, we don't have many restaurateurs on the town council."

"The facts are all in black and white," Jamie said. "We couldn't have made the report any more clear." The very next day after the emergency meeting, he and Grace had presented the council with all the data from his initial research as well as a consolidation of why his proposal would be better suited to Tuckers Bluff than Crocker. "The pub will be a boom all around for the county. Not only by bringing in new customers for all the shops, but by selling local wines from Brady—something I wouldn't count on Hemingway's to do—and having local baked goods—"

Toni waved a fork at him, "Just remember, if business gets too good you're going to need more than me."

"Noted." He grinned at his cousin's wife.

"The problem is some of the more vocal folks on the council want to go with the fast money." Grace took a sip of her beer. "This is pretty good. What is it again?"

"Dallas Craft," Jamie answered quickly. "That's the brewery expanding and seriously considering bringing their business out here if we open O'Fearadaigh's."

"Don't companies want to move into Dallas, not away from it?" Aunt Eileen asked.

"That's mostly companies coming from high tax states. Which is the reason Dave, the brewery owner, wants to move some place less hectic."

"No one would ever describe Tuckers Bluff as hectic." Abbie smiled.

"Dallas is growing so fast some people think it's going to be another Los Angeles soon. Dave and his wife just had their second child. Small town living is holding a lot more appeal for them than it might have a couple of years ago."

Eileen slathered butter on a piece of roll and, rather than toss it into her mouth, studied it. "Maybe we need to show the council more than a report."

"Explain, please," Sean prodded his sister-in-law.

"Do we know anyone who bakes better than Toni?"

Jamie shook his head. "Which is why I promised her my first born to bake the bread for the pub."

"Exactly." Eileen waved the buttered morsel at her nephew.

"Even though I follow the recipe to the letter, and even though my soda bread is mouthwatering good, when Toni follows the recipe it's like stepping into my grandmother's kitchen again. Only the few of us here have ever tasted Toni's soda bread."

"Or her rolls," Meg added.

"Which," Abbie held one up, "are really good."

"You've got a point." The family patriarch looked to Aunt Eileen. "Please make it."

Aunt Eileen rolled her eyes and faced her nephew. "Like Doubting Thomas, the council needs to see exactly what they'll be getting."

Doubting Thomas? Staring at his aunt's wide grin the connection suddenly clicked in his mind. "Or," he smiled back at her, "taste."

"We'll invite the council to the ranch," Aunt Eileen continued, "cook everything on the menu for them."

For the first time in days he felt a glimmer of hope. He hadn't voiced his fears out loud, but with every passing day that the council delayed coming out in his favor, the dream of a family pub had been slipping away, but now…

"You may have something," Jamie said. "After all, the way to a man's heart is through his stomach,"

"Oh," Meg bounced in her seat, "I'm liking this. Do you think it might be better to invite them here in town to the B&B, maybe include a few other folks also to get a resident's take on the menu?"

"That's a great idea." Adam patted his wife's knee under the table. "The ranch may be a bit like we're all ganging up on the council, but hosting a meal here in town may help them feel more like they're on their home turf."

"Well," Abbie cleared her throat, "if you're looking for neutral territory you can do this at the café. We can close it off to regular customers, just invite the council and a few special invitation guests. Even though that's a great kitchen, a commercial kitchen would work more in your favor."

Everyone at the table stared at Abbie. A few mouths even hung slightly open.

Abbie looked from left to right and shrugged. “What can I say, I’ve been convinced the pub will be good for this town.”

Until now, Jamie hadn’t been sure he’d made any real progress convincing Abbie, only suspected. Knowing she was on his side for sure, he couldn’t stop himself from grinning like the village idiot.

One by one, each family member at the table smiled and nodded.

“Sounds like we have a plan.” Aunt Eileen leaned back, rubbing her hands together.

“Agreed,” Sean tapped a spoon lightly on the table, “but what if we go one better.”

“One better?” Jamie asked.

Uncle Sean nodded. “Invite Hemingway’s to come and do the same.”

It took Jamie a moment to connect the dots. A deep rumble of laughter erupted at the thought of the mayor and his cronies champing down on sushi and BLTs made with eggplant instead of bacon. “Oh, that’s rich, Uncle Sean.”

“I know.” The man laughed with him.

“But it could work,” Meg added.

“Not could.” Aunt Eileen bobbed her head. “Side by side, you’ll beat Hemingway’s hands down.”

“Especially,” Adam added, “if you open it up to the whole town.”

“Like a fair?” Meg asked.

“Or,” Eileen grinned splitting her face in two, “a sort of cook-off. This needs to be bigger than the town council.”

Jamie turned to Abbie. “Now that we’re turning this into the tasting to end all tastings, you still volunteering your place?”

Abbie nodded. “How can I go wrong if the whole town will be coming?”

“It will be standing room only,” Grace said cheerily. “I’ll

make the offer to Crocker and if they're on board, we'll present the proposal to the council."

"And if Crocker doesn't want to play?" Adam asked.

"Then," Jamie leaned back in his chair, excitement burning once again inside him, "we won't have the satisfaction of watching the council cringe at eggplant pizza, but either way, by the time we're done feeding them, they won't have any choice than give us the permits."

Abbie looked at him and for the first time in days her smile reached all the way to her eyes. Oh, yeah. Things were most definitely back on track.

• • • •

"You sure you want to let us do this to you?" From the driver side of his old pickup, Jamie cast a quick glance in Abbie's direction.

"You're not doing anything to me." Ever since she'd first volunteered the café during dinner at the B&B, she kept expecting that unsettling sensation that would rear its ugly head in the pit of her stomach whenever she'd made a stupid decision she would live to regret to snap at her. So far nothing had happened. From the moment she'd suggested using her kitchen she'd felt only a sense of accomplishment. Almost as if the pub was hers. Maybe it was some silly kinship after sorting through the attic of the soon to be pub. Or perhaps it had something to do with listening to Jamie's infectious enthusiasm for over a week. Whatever the reason, she very badly wanted to do this. To be a part of convincing the town council, and maybe the town too, that O'Fearadaigh's was a good idea.

Jamie turned the corner and looked her way again. "You really are one helluva woman." His eyes momentarily widened and she had the feeling he hadn't meant to say that. "I mean, uhm. Well, thank you. The town council has to take this whole thing more seriously if you're on board."

"I am. On board that is." Ideas had been popping into her

head left and right since dessert and hadn't stopped. She twisted in her seat to fully face him. "As a matter of fact, how close are you to the beer guy, is it Dave?"

Jamie nodded. "Pretty friendly. I've known him since the days when he used to hit all the local bars pimping his product himself."

"Do you think if we invited him to town for the taste off he might be keen on coming and serving his beers?"

Jamie's face brightened and that lazy smile that could make a girl weak in the knees appeared, making her very thankful she was already sitting down. "I think that's a fantastic idea. We'll give the council, and the town, the full effect of what O'Fearadaigh's will be like."

"If you're talking full effect, you'll have to do it all, food, drink, ambiance."

"Ambiance?"

"That would be Irish music too."

She didn't think his eyes could twinkle any brighter, but they did. "I should have thought of that."

"Yes." She turned forward in the seat and tugged at the safety belt, swallowing a teasing grin. "You should have." Deep down in her bones she knew this was going to work. The town council would have to be out of their ever-loving minds not to choose the Farraday's family pub over some new wave urban restaurant.

"Here you are." Jamie pulled up to the curb. As he'd done on the other nights he drove her home from work, he circled the hood of the truck in nearly the same amount of time it took her to unsnap her seatbelt and climb down to the sidewalk.

"Thanks." She'd given up on convincing him she could walk herself home without need of an escort. The routine was pretty standard. He'd walk her to the door, she'd tell him that wouldn't be necessary, he'd smile and do it anyway. Then she'd offer him tea or coffee and he would politely decline. A familiar song and dance. The lock undone, the knob turned, the door slightly ajar, she spun about to face him.

He stepped in closer than his usual spot at the edge of her porch. Close enough that she could see the flecks of gold in his eyes shining against the overhead light, and held out the two photographs for her. “Don’t forget these.”

Sea green eyes remained fixed on hers. Slowly lifting one hand, his finger gently grazed her cheek before tucking a loose strand of hair behind her ear. Her mouth went dry and her palms grew damp. It had been way too long since she’d been kissed, and Jamie Farraday had the look of a man about to do just that. Unsure if she should lean in and enjoy the moment or turn and run for the hills, her choices vanished with his single step in retreat. Once again, Jamie stood at his designated spot by the edge of the landing.

“Would you like to come in for a cup of tea or coffee? Maybe a cold drink?”

He smiled, taking another step back onto the walkway. “I’d better not. It’s late.”

“Yes.” She shoved the door behind her fully open, crossed the threshold and turned to face him. “See you tomorrow.”

“Tomorrow,” he nodded.

As she’d done all the other nights he’d brought her home, she turned the single lock, leaned against the door and waited for the rumble of the truck to disappear down the street. The difference, tonight, she wished more than ever that he would have stayed. At least a little while. And maybe, just maybe, left her with the memory of a good night kiss.

CHAPTER TEN

"Remind me again why I'm tagging along on this venture?" Sally May climbed into one of the Farraday ranch pickup trucks.

"Because," Eileen waited with a bit less patience than she should have, "if I show up on Mabel Berkner's doorstep by myself, she'll know something's up."

"Oh, right." Sally May snapped the seatbelt in place, then looked up at her friend. "And having two of us who never cross her doorway show up will be totally not suspicious."

Eileen shrugged. Maybe Sally May was right. If Eileen couldn't persuade Mabel to back off and be more supportive of what was good for the town, namely O'Fearadaigh's Public House, then as a somewhat disinterested third party, Sally May could take a shot at the old bitty. If neither succeeded, at least Sally could be counted on to either prevent Eileen from killing the high and mighty teetotaler or help Eileen bury the body.

"Uh oh. You've got that Lucy-look to you." Sally May shifted on the passenger side of the massive quad cab. "The one that always gets Ethel into trouble."

"Nonsense. Just planning my speech ahead silently."

"Uh huh." Her friend of a bazillion years blew out a sigh. "Okay, what's the strategy and what's my role?"

"I'm still working on that part."

"What?" Sally May swiveled around to face her again.

"Well, I haven't yet come up with the right angle. Something to make her, if not support Jamison, at least not fight us."

"We could talk down California hippy liberalism."

"Is Hemingway's based in California? And do they still have hippies?"

"No idea, but I'm guessing she doesn't know either. That woman could make a right wing conservative seem downright communist. You gotta know she won't like anything that even hints at alfalfa sprouts or tofu or free love or legal pot."

"Yeah, well, I'm pretty sure free love and legal pot won't be on Hemingway's menus."

Sally May looked over the rim of her sunglasses. "And alfalfa?"

"Maybe." Eileen wished now she'd taken more time to learn about Hemingway's before heading off to take on Mabel. "Jamie does seem to mention eggplant a lot."

"Ooh, eggplant parmesan is really good."

"I don't think they cook Italian. I'm pretty sure Jamie referred to it on a hamburger, or was that a club sandwich?"

Sally May's face scrunched in horror. "Either way, ick."

"See. That's why this cook-off is such a great idea. As long as Hemingway's doesn't cook rib eyes and baked potatoes, we're golden."

"Then why do we need Mabel on board?"

"Because I'd rather be platinum."

Sally May rolled her eyes and shook her head.

Mabel Berkner lived on the other side of town about twenty minutes past the old golf course. The woman never married and as far as anyone knew only had the one nephew, her sister Lilly's boy. Not the brightest bulb in the chandelier.

By the time Eileen pulled into the long narrow drive leading to the house that had been in Mabel's family for generations, neither she nor Sally May had come up with a solid plan.

"This is absolutely crazy." Sally May climbed down from the truck, mumbling. "It will never work."

"Oh, shush." Eileen slammed the driver side door shut. Deep down she feared her friend was right, but that was the last thing she wanted to admit. The Farradays had a lot riding on the upcoming cook-off. This crazy effort had to work. It just had to.

The second Eileen's foot hit the ground the sound of barking dogs slammed into her. Glancing around, Eileen was delighted to see the two animals snarling like junkyard dogs were kenneled.

"Wouldn't want to run into one of those two in a dark alley on a cold dark night." Sally May frowned at the snarling animals. "So help me, if I wind up with a backside full buckshot on account of this house call, you will pay."

"Nonsense."

No sooner had the words escaped Eileen's mouth then the front door of Berkner homestead creaked open. Eileen half expected to see the business end of a shotgun greet her. Relief washed over her at the sight of Mabel offering a wary smile.

"Now, since when do you two make afternoon calls?"

Afternoon call? This woman really was living in the last century. Gentlemen callers and afternoon social visits had long ago fallen by the wayside along with prohibition and suffragettes. "I've been thinking it's time to redo the kitchen at the ranch house, and Sister tells me you've recently redone yours. Thought you might be willing to show me what you did."

"Kitchen?" Mabel's expression faltered briefly. "That was nearly five years ago."

"Then I guess it's time we saw it." Sally May came to a stop beside Eileen. "I hear it can make a person's mouth water."

Times like this it really paid off to have sneaky friends who could take a short lead and lie like a rug. The kitchen excuse was pretty lame. If Eileen had thought about it she would have realized it had indeed been years since the sisters mentioned Mabel had dropped a pretty penny on a fancy new kitchen. Which at the time had made no sense since they were pretty sure Mabel didn't like to cook.

"Sisters couldn't stop talking about it." This was the part where Eileen hoped Sister and Sissy had actually seen the kitchen remodel. And judging from the bright smile that bloomed across Mabel's face, Eileen was pretty sure Mabel had bought their story, hook, line and sinker.

"I'm afraid the house is a bit of a mess." Still grinning, Mabel shoved aside a couple of large boxes stacked along the hallway. In the kitchen a few more boxes were lined against the inside wall.

"Are you going somewhere?" Sally May frowned down at an open box.

Taking two Mason jars off the kitchen island and slipping them into the empty spaces in the top box, Mabel quickly closed the lid and spun around. "Thought I'd give another shot at canning vegetables and using my great granny's recipe for preserves."

Eileen nodded. With most of the family moved out and on their own, Eileen's vegetable garden was a fraction of the size it had been when the kids were growing up, and yet she still had enough canned goods in the pantry to survive a nuclear meltdown.

"As you can see," Mabel waived an arm from one side of the kitchen to the other, "this is not my grandmother's kitchen."

There was no denying that. Sleek mid-century, or would that be Scandinavian, cabinets lined three walls. Stunning solid surface countertops made this place a baker's dream. Eileen was no expert on appliances, but any fool could see the huge stainless steel range was commercial grade, and the double built-in fridge was one of those insanely expensive custom models.

"I would kill for a full fridge." Eileen opened the refrigerator side of the appliance and peered inside. She had one of those French door refrigerators that gave her a good amount of space, but never enough.

Mabel patted the freezer side door. "Can't imagine going back to having my freezer in the mudroom again."

Both Eileen and Sally May moved around the kitchen oohing and ahing, lovingly stroking the marble counters and custom cabinets.

"Would you look at these?" Sally May fingered the cabinet handles. "If these aren't the cutest things. Forks and spoons, I love it."

Mabel beamed as though someone had just told her she'd won an international beauty pageant. "That was my idea. Found them online and knew they would be perfect for that little bit of country feel."

Little just about covered it, because there was nothing else about this kitchen that said country. Eileen knew the Berkner family had always been well-off, but she didn't realize how well-off until now. She wasn't a builder, but she knew enough about pricing a kitchen remodel to know this kitchen had to have cost Mabel what some young folks pay for a new starter home in these parts.

"I struggled between quartz and marble." Mabel ran her hand across the Carrara counters. "But in the end the marble just looked so pretty."

"That it does." Sally May pulled one of the stools out from under the island and took a seat. "I could do some serious baking on this sucker."

Eileen dropped a fisted hand on one hip. "When was the last time you baked?"

"Don't know, but for this counter, I take it up again."

The three women laughed. Probably the first time Eileen could ever remember Mabel Berkner not looking like she'd sucked on a lemon.

"Shall I put on a pot of tea, or do you ladies want to just tell me why you're really here?"

Eileen shot Sally May a sideways glance before focusing on Mabel. "I really did want to see this kitchen. I have no idea how old the ranch kitchen is, but older than me is a fair guess."

"And…?" Mabel took a seat, smiling, but shaking her head. "If you think you can flatter me into not protesting the new liquor license laws, it's not going to work."

"How much do you know about the establishment that Jamison and the family want to open?"

"I don't need to know the details to know this town has done very well for itself in a dry county. We don't have a lot of drunk and disorderly behavior, no trouble with teenagers getting all liquored up in a field. Having to drive all the way to Butler Springs for a six pack of beer, never mind a bottle of whiskey, has kept our town nice and peaceful, just the way we like it."

"It's not like Jamie is going to be serving every teenager in town whiskey." Eileen threw her arms up.

Sally May raised a finger at Mabel. "And it's not like they can't find homemade hooch closer to home."

"We've never had a problem with teenagers partying on local moonshine."

"That we know of."

"Seriously, Eileen," Mabel said. "You don't think your nephew, the chief of police, would say something if we had a problem with teenagers getting drunk on moonshine the way underage teens can buy booze in the big cities and hang out the back seat of cars or empty fields until they make themselves sick?"

"I agree." Eileen nodded. "We don't have a problem with drunken behavior, and letting the pub open isn't going to change that."

"It's a slippery slope. One establishment opens and then another and then another and before you know anyone can buy liquor at a grocery store or a gas station. Eventually there could be more places to buy booze than coffee in this town."

Eileen pushed to her feet. "Now Mabel, you're exaggerating. Not only is this town not going to turn into sin city because of one Irish pub, but the town is only going to issue one liquor license."

"One?" The old biddy looked truly surprised.

Eileen nodded. "One. And Hemingway's is fighting awfully hard for it to be their establishment that gets it."

"And how does this affect me?" The sourpuss expression had returned to Mabel's face.

"At least O'Fearadaigh's will be looking out for their own. We care about this town as much as you do. And those West Coast corporate types only care about the bottom line."

Mabel's gaze narrowed. Eileen couldn't tell if the woman was on the verge of agreeing or disagreeing, or getting ready to blow her top or give in.

"We can be sure," Eileen continued, "that the pub would

serve the local wine from the Brady's vineyard, local baked goods, local raised beef, and Jamie's working really hard to get a craft beer company to move their operations out here. You don't need me to tell you how much good it would do a town to get a handful of new families in our school system, shopping in our stores, buying our vacant properties and sprucing them up."

Mabel continued to stare silently, her lips pressed in a thin line. Eileen didn't like the looks of it. Maybe coming here wasn't as good an idea as she'd thought. Maybe Sally May was right and there's no convincing this old bag to change her antiquated way of thinking.

"Well," Eileen stood up. "I've said my piece, hoping you'd consider working with the Farraday's for this town and not against us. But either way, we'll keep working to fight for this pub and fight hard. There's plenty of business to be brought in from around the county and new business is good for Tuckers Bluff."

Sally May pushed away from the counter and nodded at Mabel. "I know how you feel Mabel, but we can't stop the world from changing."

The sour expression on Mabel's face remained intact. Without a word she escorted the two guests to the front door.

"Thank you for letting us look at the kitchen." Eileen turned on the front porch to face Mabel. "It really is everything the sisters said it was."

A hint of a smile tugged at one side of Mabel's face. "Thank you, ladies."

Two feet off the front porch, Eileen noticed the small vegetable garden to her right. Looking over her shoulder at Mabel still standing in the open doorway, she pointed to the vegetables and hollered, "You may want to plant some marigolds in there. That will stop the garden pest problem you've got going here."

Mabel shifted her attention to the sorry looking garden in the front yard and then back to Eileen. "I'll keep that in mind. Thank you."

Not till the engine had started and they'd turned back onto the driveway did Mabel close the door.

"Well that went well." Sally May forced a smile. "At least you didn't make me tie her to a chair and lock her in the closet until all the decision-making is over."

"Oh for heaven's sake. There's no need to exaggerate." Eileen pulled onto the main road toward town.

"I'll tell you something else, as good as that woman can be at making trouble for us, she's equally going to be as bad at canning vegetables. If that woman manages to get a week worth of food stored, I'll dance naked down Main Street."

"Oh heck no. I'd better get myself over to Mabel's and help her fix that vegetable garden."

"That puny thing? The woman hasn't a clue what she's doing."

The two women cracked up laughing. Truth was they were both in pretty good condition for women of their age. Neither of them had the svelte figures they'd had in their twenties, but working a ranch most of their lives had kept them in good enough shape.

"Do you really think having Mabel on our side would make much of a difference?" Sally May asked.

Eileen cast a last look at the Berkner homestead fading in the distance. "I honestly don't know. But if she insists on protesting, I sure as heck hope not."

CHAPTER ELEVEN

Almost another full week under his belt and Jamie was starting to feel like he was getting the hang of this running a kitchen thing. He wouldn't have wished injury on anyone, but Frank's hurting his foot was turning out to be a pretty good learning lesson for Jamie. What hadn't been so easy was keeping a safe distance from Abbie. As much as he admired Frank, every day, the more he learned about Abbie the more amazing she was to him. In the short drives home, he'd learned she was an only child who had lost her parents nearly a decade ago, she loved helping people, blueberry pie, and she painted flowers because she had a brown thumb. The first week after driving her home, out of sheer respect for how tired she had to be, he'd turned down the invitation for a late night cup of coffee. By the second week he'd said no simply because he wanted so badly to say yes.

Tying a knot on the black garbage bag, he opened the rear door and only made it two steps when a familiar fuzzy blur bolted at him from behind the trash cans.

Dropping the bag on the ground, Jamie squatted just as the puppy leapt at him, knocking him flat on his butt. "You really have to stop doing this to people," he laughed, scratching behind the dog's ears.

Oblivious to Jamie's admonishment, the fuzzball happily licked his face, squirming in place.

"Okay, okay, calm down." Jamie shifted, getting a better grip on the dog. "What I'd like to know is who you belong to that keeps letting you out loose."

Pup barked a single yap response.

The sound of Jamie's name drifted through the open doorway.

"I'm out here."

Abbie stood in the doorway, the light filtering behind her like a halo. "What is this?"

"We have company." Jamie sputtered through laughter.

No longer interested in Jamie, the pup scooted over to where Abbie stood.

"Aren't you just adorable?" Squatting on her haunches, she scratched under his chin with one hand and rubbed his back with the other. "Who do you belong to?"

"I was just asking him the same thing. Whoever it is really shouldn't let him out on his own like this to get into more trouble."

Lifting her gaze away from the dog, Abbie focused on Jamie. "More trouble?"

Jamie nodded. "With all the commotion and concern after Frank's injury, I may not have mentioned this little guy was the reason Frank fell off the ladder."

Her voice soft and low and sweet, Abbie lifted the dog's nose to her face. "I really should be very annoyed with you for what you've done to my cook. But you're too adorable to be angry with."

A long lick, straight from chin to nose was the puppy's response.

"Okay." Abbie coughed and rubbed around her mouth. "You're not that adorable."

Her face all scrunched, Jamie thought she looked absolutely adorable as well. "Do you suppose he's astray? Maybe Frank had been feeding him?"

"That's doubtful. Frank probably would've said something to us when he fell off the ladder." Abbie continued to scratch and pet the puppy now sitting perfectly still, his eyes glazing over with delight.

Lucky dog, Jamie thought. And *that* was why he'd yet to accept an offer of late night coffee.

Abbie lifted her gaze from the puppy to Jamie. "I have to ask Frank if he'd noticed someone getting into the trash."

"Nothing's been out of the ordinary since I've been working

the kitchen. Tonight's the first time I've seen any sign of him. I had just assumed he'd gone home to whoever his owners were and hadn't gotten out again."

"Well he doesn't look like he's very hungry. I know he's not wearing a collar, but maybe he has a chip."

"That's a great idea. We can take him to Adam to scan for a chip. Find out who the owner is and let him know that the puppy keeps getting into trouble."

"That's not true." Abbie lifted the pup's nose to her face again, not as close as last time. "You're not in any trouble."

"Babies and puppies." Jamie rolled his eyes to the night sky and back.

Abbie kept her attention on the soft fuzzball. "What about them?"

"They can do no wrong." He chuckled and reached out to scratch the other ear. He certainly wasn't going to tell her that at the ranch all it took was one cute baby to turn all of his cousins into goofy sweet-talking babbling halfwits. Pushing to his feet, he brushed his hands clean. "Are we done for the night?"

Abbie stood up and nodded. "Last customer just left. Grace and her husband are inside. She's heard from Crocker."

"At this late hour?"

"Guess it's not too late to be working in California."

Leaning sideways Jamie looked over her shoulder into the kitchen. "Good or bad?"

"She didn't say."

"Then let's get this over with." Jamie looked down at his feet, first left then right. "Where did he go?"

Abbie spun around a full three hundred and sixty degrees. "I don't see him."

"He has to be around here somewhere." He grabbed the trash bag, carried it over to the garbage bins, watching every step for the dog. "A regular Houdini."

Walking a few feet away from the door, around and back, Abbie shook her head. "No sign of him."

"I really would like to know who that animal belongs to, but I've got more important things to look after right now." Letting his hand fall on the small of Abbie's back, he nudged her inside, through the kitchen, and pushed the double doors open.

Abbie shifted to one side. "I'll finish cleaning up."

"Uh uh." Jamie shook his head. "You're as much a part of this now as I am. We'll both hear what Grace has to say."

Abbie hesitated a brief moment before nodding. Placing his hand at the small of her back again, he walked with her to the booth where Grace and her husband were seated waiting. He liked the feel of Abbie under his fingertips. The warmth of her standing beside him. Yep, he definitely liked the feel of her just a little too much.

• • • •

"It's official, we're on." Grace practically bounced from her seat.

Abbie wished they'd chosen a table and not a booth to sit in. She wasn't sure sitting so close to Jamie was very smart. Already she missed the warmth of Jamie's gentle touch. How ridiculous was that? With no choice, she slid in across from Grace and her husband.

"Are you talking Council approval, or Crocker's?" Jamie slid in beside Abbie.

Grace laid both hands flat on the table in front of her. "I mean the new restaurant cook-off is official. Not only has the town council approved the idea, but Crocker has agreed to participate."

"How about that." Jamie hefted one shoulder in a halfhearted shrug. "I wasn't sure if they'd get on board with the idea."

"Well," Grace rubbed her hands together enthusiastically. "I may have eluded that the only way to attain the liquor license would be to participate."

"You didn't?" Abbie didn't want to think how much trouble they'd get in if the truth came out.

"I did not." Smiling, Grace leaned back in the booth. "I

merely chose my words carefully, how they interpreted those words is not my fault."

Both Chase and Jamie barked with laughter.

"You certainly do make life fun." Chase squeezed his wife's hand, giving her a quick peck on the lips.

"So," Grace addressed her question to Jamie, "who is going to do the cooking for O'Fearadaigh's?"

"That would be me." Jamie pointed a thumb at himself.

Abbie shook her head. "I know this is none of my business—"

"You bet it's your business," Jamie interrupted.

"While I'll agree I have something at stake here. How you run this is really up to the family, but I do think the cooking shouldn't be on you. Your job should be to win the townspeople over, to schmooze the town council, to just be a Farraday."

"Don't you have a cook lined up?" Chase asked.

"Had one lined up. Things have changed a bit, and Brad couldn't turn down another offer."

Grace pressed her lips together in a moment of thought. "This is going to be a family business. It only makes sense to have the family involved, at least in the cooking for the competition. Do you at least have the menu?"

"Absolutely." Jamie nodded. "Right down to Mom's Irish Stew."

Grace's eyes opened wide. "She shared the recipe?"

"Apparently she and Aunt Eileen have reached out to every distant relative we have from here to the Emerald Isle itself gathering recipes."

Hand over her mouth, Abbie did her best to hold back a smile. How she loved that woman. If she could only pick one person in this world to have her back, it would be Aunt Eileen. As much as she loved and trusted DJ, his aunt had her vote hands down.

"Good. We'll do it like those food festivals in any major city except it will all be free. Guests can taste a little of this and a little of that."

"Appetizers, main meal, dessert." Jamie nodded, the smile at the corners of his mouth slowly lifting higher and higher. “We’ll wipe ‘em up.”

“What about drinks?” Abbie asked. “Any way to get a special dispensation or something to serve beer?”

Grace nodded. “Yes. I can’t believe I forgot to mention it. Each company will be issued a single day one time permit to serve the liquor.”

Turning to face Jamie, Abbie shouldn’t have been surprised to see him already looking at her smiling and nodding. He didn’t need to say a word; she already knew what he was thinking. The next call he would make would be to the Dallas brewery.

Twenty minutes later, inside the future Farraday’s pub, final design plans scrolled open atop a makeshift table of plywood and sawhorses, Abbie stood listening to Jamie’s side of the conversation.

“Uh huh, that’s right, two weeks.” Jamie straightened, shifting his attention from the blueprints to the pegboard walls across the room. “Good, good. We’d love to have you. Appreciate your getting right on this.” Nodding his head and holding the phone to one ear, Jamie’s grin grew. His left arm bumped casually against her, his fingers quickly weaved through hers and he squeezed her hand.

Excited at the sparkle in his eye as he continued to bob his head at whatever Dave had to say, it took Abbie a few moments to notice Jamie had not let go of her hand. The giddy feeling of a young teen catching the attention of the good-looking nice guy on campus flooded her unexpectedly.

“Sounds perfect. We’ll see you tomorrow.” The conversation over, Jamie let go of her hand, swiped to disconnect the call, and slid the phone into his pocket before turning to face her. “Dave and his wife are going to drive out here tomorrow. They’ll check out the town, the café, and this place. That is, what there is of it.”

A sliver of disappointment nipped momentarily at her good mood. Jamie gave no indication that holding her hand had been anything more than an enthusiastic impulse. Deep down she’d instinctively known not to make anything of the gesture. And even if she'd wanted to feel sorry for herself for at least a minute or two, she couldn't. The air around them fizzled with excitement as every inch of their plans came together. Well, his plans. "Are they only staying the day?"

Jamie shook his head. "He'll stay at least the weekend at the B&B. He's calling Meg now."

"All right then." Abbie slapped her hands together and surveyed the empty space. She'd known Jamie had been coming to clean out the main storefront most nights after dropping her off, but hadn't realized how much progress he'd made. Too wound up over Grace's good news, tonight she had insisted on joining Jamie with the cleanup. "Where do we start?"

"Down here is just waiting for demolition once we get the go ahead with the permits. I've also gone through all the boxes upstairs of old ledgers and outdated paperwork. Most of it was trash but I did take some to Marion."

"Oh, I bet she liked that."

Jamie chuckled. "Actually, she did. That woman has quite a fondness for old paper."

"I bet."

"Anyhow, I haven't touched any of the trunks upstairs yet." His gaze dropped to the floor before lifting to meet her eyes. His bright smile appeared a tad bit shaky, and a hint of color reached his face. "I had sort of hoped you might want to sort through those with me."

The same giddy feeling that had rushed through her when he held her hand came hurrying back. She didn't know what to make of all the emotions working their way to the surface or the sweet way Jamie had been treating her, but for once in her life she wasn't going to think something to death and was determined to simply enjoy the ride.

CHAPTER TWELVE

Right about now more than anything else, Jamie wished he could read Abbie's mind. Her pleased smile gave no indication if it was his gesture of waiting for her that gave her pleasure, or simply the prospect of digging through history again.

"I'd like that." Abbie waved him on. "I'd offer to race you, but I don't think we can afford any more mis-steps."

"Definitely not." He resisted the urge to reach out and take hold of her hand again. When he'd done so earlier on the phone it had been sheer instinct that had him reaching out for her. Then when he realized he still held on, he did his best to casually let go and hoped he hadn't scared her away. At this point he was merely delighted she wasn't annoyed with him and would be working at his side. "It occurred to me that the upstairs space would actually be really good for some offices. Maybe use some of that furniture." He tugged the rope, lowering the foldout stairs.

"Oh, that sounds great. Have you told the architect to draw in a real staircase? The kind that doesn't descend from a ceiling?"

"Won't need the architect for that. A cousin or two and I could build them in an afternoon."

Grabbing hold of the rails and taking one step up, she turned to look at him over her shoulder. "For the record, I won't object if y'all start on that any day now."

"I'll do that," he chuckled, "but I suspect you'd get faster action out of my cousins if you did the asking. Not that they don't want to help me, but an attic staircase is not on anyone's priority list." He started up the ladder behind her.

At the top, dusting off her hands, she turned to face him. "I just might do that."

They'd barely reached the top of the stairs when he heard voices calling "yoo hoo" in the distance. "Did you hear that?"

Hands on her hips, Abbie leaned toward the attic opening. The voices sounding once again. "Yep. Women's voices. Are you expecting someone else?"

Jamie shook his head.

"Olly olly oxen free," sounded louder and more clearly accompanied by more than one female voice giggling.

"They have to be here somewhere," another woman announced.

"I bet they're upstairs." This time Jamie recognized his aunt.

"Uh oh." Wide eyed, Abbie spun to face him. "I may be wrong, but my first guess is that the girls' Friday night-out has just been moved from Meg's house to here."

"Why here?" he asked.

Footsteps came to a halt at the bottom of the stairs. "Yoo hoo."

"I think we're about to find out." Abbie laughed and crossed the attic to the stairway opening. "We're up here. Come on and join the party."

Leading the pack, Meg was first up the stairs. One by one Jamie's family and friends followed her onto the second floor.

"Just got off the phone a little bit ago with Dave," Meg started. "He and his wife will be arriving tomorrow, but you already know that." She turned from Jamie to Abbie. "And Grace said y'all closed a little early tonight. Since you're not answering your phone and your house is pitch black and Dave said Jamie was here at the pub location, we figured you must be here too."

"Sorry, my phone is on silent in my purse downstairs."

Becky maneuvered around her sister-in-law. "No matter, we found you." DJ's wife smiled with a little bit more enthusiasm than he was used to even for her.

"Yep." Aunt Eileen came around scanning the area as she spoke. "Since Mohammed won't come to the mountain, we figured we'd bring the mountain to Mohammed. Hey," she pointed behind

Abbie, "is that a Lincoln rocker?"

Before Jamie could fully process a gaggle of women all talking at once, the storage room had been transformed from dusty mayhem to party hall. One of the trunks had been cleared off to use as a tabletop for several bottles of wine, plates of snacks and Toni's—he suspected fully boozed—cake balls. He'd never seen all these ladies quite so… happy.

Not usually a man slow to react, still standing frozen in the same spot since everyone had climbed upstairs, Jamie didn't know what to do next. His aunt and a few others buzzed about like bees from flower to flower, savoring every new find. Dusting off a discovery of velvet covered folding chairs, Toni and Becky scattered them around the trunk turned coffee table.

Squeezing her way between Meg and Grace, Abbie worked her way back toward him. "You look a little stunned."

"Let's just say, this wasn't what I expected to be doing at this hour on a Friday night." He glanced around at the smiling happy faces. "But everyone seems a little bit too happy."

Abbie let out a deep chuckle. "Don't underestimate them. Sure they've had a glass of wine or two—"

"Two?"

"Mostly," she smiled, "but what you're watching is the synergy of women taking care of women. Everyone works long and hard, day after day, week after week, and girls' night is their chance to enjoy and recharge."

On second look, he realized she was right. While an inordinate amount of laughter abounded all around him, the conversation was practical, clear, and reminded him of a birthday party for his sister when she was a little girl. A dozen or more friends gathered with cake and ice cream, laughing, giggling, having the time of their lives and all of them obviously perfectly sober.

"Jamie," someone called from across the attic, "you're going to have to use some of these pictures in the pub."

"Synergy," he mumbled.

"The best kind." Abbie waved for him to follow her. "Come on. Let's go see what treasures they've come across."

Jamie nodded. He'd join in on the fun tonight, but he wasn't interested in treasure. He was pretty sure he'd already found his, and for now, would follow her anywhere.

• • • •

"Wow, I can't believe how much stuff is crammed in that attic." Abbie collapsed on the sofa, propping her feet up on the coffee table.

Meg sank into the oversized easy chair beside Abbie. "You're not kidding. I hope Jamie takes me seriously when I tell him I'd love to have a few of those pieces for the B&B."

"Most of it, except for a century of dirt, is in pretty good shape." Aunt Eileen leaned back on the other end of the sofa.

"Well," Catherine, Connor's wife, dropped her purse on the floor. "Since I'm the only one still standing, I guess I'll put on the kettle for tea."

"You don't have to do that." Abbie swung one foot off the table.

Aunt Eileen's arm came across and she patted Abbie on the knee. "Let her. You've been on your feet all day and most of the night."

"She's right," Catherine said. "I sit at a desk all day long. Let someone else take care of you for a minute."

"I'll admit, the concept holds great appeal." With the crazy hours Abbie always kept it was rare she'd have company at her house. It was even more unusual for her to be included on a Friday night outing, but once in a blue moon, like tonight, the dinner crowd would taper off unusually early and she'd get home at a decent hour. Not that 12:30 in the morning was a decent hour, but the gang had spent the last few hours sifting through all the remnants of yesteryear and Tuckers Bluff.

"I'm a little surprised that Jamie lasted as long as he did,"

Meg mumbled through a yawn.

Aunt Eileen waved her finger at her niece-in-law. "None of that. Don't get us started."

"You have to admit, not many a man can hold his own around that many women."

"We did have an unusually large turnout tonight, didn't we?" Aunt Eileen said.

Abbie smiled. "I'm glad I got to play with everyone tonight."

"I know I've said this before," Meg sat forward, "but you could consider hiring a part-time waitress to give you a couple of nights off a week."

Catherine came into the room carrying a tray of cups and saucers and other teatime accessories. "One night a week would be a start. Surely you could do one night a week?"

More than once the thought had crossed Abbie's mind that it was time to slow down, to stop pushing so hard. Her mind didn't wander back to ugly places as often as it used to, then she'd come home to an empty quiet house with nothing more to look forward to than an occasional run to the store or a few hours dabbling with paints, and think maybe next year.

The teakettle sounded and Catherine scurried into the kitchen, calling over her shoulder, "No one discussed the elephant in the room tonight."

Sitting up, placing teabags and mugs and adding sugar and milk and casting sideways glances at each other, no one said a word.

"We really should hedge our bets." Catherine returned, teakettle in hand and began pouring into each person's cup. "I know everybody was having fun picking out pictures and other items to display at the new pub, and that the family has been discussing recipes for the menu, and we've got the craft beer guy coming to town tomorrow, but we've got less than two weeks to pull this off and I think we need more of a plan."

Aunt Eileen dipped her teabag in and out of the boiling water. "Sally May and I went to go visit Mabel Berkner."

"Really?" Abbie wasn't sure what to make of that little bit of news.

"She is, after all, the most vocal opponent to the pub."

Catherine took a seat. "She's opposed to anybody selling booze. And yes, she is the most vocal."

"My thought was," Aunt Eileen stirred her hot brew, "if we could get her on our side somehow that might mean more to the town council."

Meg blew on her tea. "I don't understand why she would want to support either option."

"Better the devil you know than the devil you don't." Abbie set her teacup down on the table. "She may not like the idea of liquor in the county, but that's water under the bridge. She can balk all she wants, the folks of this county voted and the county or this town isn't changing their minds. On the other hand, if there's going to be liquor sold in Tuckers Bluff, at least she knows the Farradays are good honest people and care about this town is much as she does."

Catherine looked to Aunt Eileen. "So how did it go?"

"Not very well." Aunt Eileen paused for a sip. "Most of the time Sally May and I talked the woman looked like she'd been sucking on lemons."

Abbie laughed. "Well that doesn't mean anything. She always looks like she's sucking on lemons."

Aunt Eileen shrugged.

"Maybe we can't convince Mabel, but what about the council?" Meg said. "Maybe we can sweeten the pot a little for those who are leaning away from the pub."

"Bribe them?" Abbie couldn't believe she just heard that.

"Of course not." Meg shook her head "I was thinking of a little negotiating. You know, like lobbyists do. Or politicians."

"Comparing sweetening the pot to lobbyists and politicians is not making me feel all warm and fuzzy," Abbie said.

Aunt Eileen jetted her chin forward, rubbing under her jaw. "She may have something there. This county has gotten through some rough times for many a generation with a little horse trading. That's how barns got built and cattle and sheep ranchers learned to live side by side. Yep, I definitely think she's onto something."

"So," Catherine rubbed her hands together. "We've got less than two weeks to find out who is leaning towards giving the permit to Hemingway's and fishing out how O'Fearadaigh's could be more of a benefit to them individually as well as the town than the competition."

Aunt Eileen nodded. "I like this idea. For sure, I know from Grace the mayor is thinking there's more to be had by taking on an international company. I'll talk to Sean and see what we can do about him."

Surrounded by smiling ladies, Abbie hoped it was going to be this easy. She'd grown accustomed to the idea of having Jamie around. Not that she didn't miss working with Frank, and not that she didn't know soon enough she wouldn't get to spend as much time with Jamie. Common sense told her if the pub didn't get its license, the Farradays would find something else to do with that building but Jamie would not have any reason to stay in Tuckers Bluff. That idea, more than anything else running through her mind at the moment, bothered her way more than it should. And what the heck was she going to do about that?

CHAPTER THIRTEEN

"Ante up." Eileen tossed a chip into the pot. Morning poker games at the café had been a regular part of her routine for as long as she could remember. She had no idea how she would have survived those first few years after Helen's death without these fabulous women she called friends.

Ruth Ann waved a finger at her. "Are you planning on dealing anytime soon or you just going to shuffle the cards until dinnertime?"

"My, my, someone is testy today." Dorothy tsked at her longtime friend. "Trouble in paradise?"

Twirling the long gray braid that hung halfway down her back into a knot at the base of her neck, Ruth Ann rolled her eyes. "Not everything has to do with my love life."

"I don't know about that." Sally May shrugged. "How high you rate on a grumpy scale lately seems to be directly related to how happy you are with Ralph."

At least one of them, Eileen thought, had a love life. Until Ruth Ann started keeping company with Ralph, Eileen had considered love and relationships something tucked away in the memories of younger days.

"Ralph and I are perfectly fine." Ruth Ann waved a hand at Eileen. "She's still shuffling that deck. Much longer and she'll wear a groove in the sides."

All eyes turned to the arch of cards one by one falling flatly into place.

Dorothy raised her brows. "Ruth Ann does have a point. By now they may have been shuffled back to where they were in the beginning."

Slamming the deck in front of her dearest friend, Eileen waited for Dorothy to cut the cards. No point in saying anything, they were right, she'd been a little distracted this morning. That stupid letter that she should have simply thrown into the trash when it first arrived had come flying out of the drawer along with a clean bra. Floating to the floor, the return address boldly stared up at her, taunted her still.

"Eileen," Ruth Ann repeated.

"You planning on winning big?" Eileen did her best to cover her mind wandering—again, and gathered the deck, dealing out five cards quickly.

"Should've let you keep shuffling." Ruth Ann rearranged her cards left to right then right to left.

Eileen sorted through her own cards. Her luck is not any better than Ruth Ann's and Eileen had not had a love life in almost 30 years.

"Oh, look." Dorothy discreetly pointed toward the front of the café under her cards. "Looks like the mayor's sidekick, councilman Roy Garland, is here for lunch. Alone."

Waiting to see if anybody joined him, Eileen darted a glance over the rim of her cards a time or two.

"Well," Sally May leaned forward, "here's your chance to find out what the one of the council wants."

Ruth Ann folded her cards in front of her. "Or have you decided Sean is right and to leave well enough alone and let the chips fall where they may?"

"I hope not." Dorothy tossed aside two cards. "Like it or not, this is politics, and we can't just stand back and hope the good guy wins. The least we can do is have a nice friendly conversation with one of our town council and see what strikes his fancy."

"Agreed." Assured that the councilman was lunching alone and would welcome her company, Eileen played out the end of her hand. The timing was perfect. As she tossed the last of her cards down to the table, Donna set the mayor's lunch on the table in front of him.

"You fixing to go somewhere?" Holding a pitcher of tea in one hand and a pot of coffee and the other, Abbie came to a stop beside Eileen.

"Yep," Eileen nodded. "Cross your fingers, girls, I'm going in. Here's hoping he's as easy to con facts out of as my nephews were when they didn't want Sean and me to know what they were up to."

Sally May gathered the cards in front of her. "Oh for land sakes, he can't be as gullible as a couple of teens. Hope you've got something else up your sleeve."

"No, but you know what they say?" Eileen flashed a knowing smile. "What separates the men from the boys is the price of their toys."

• • • •

Every time Abbie walked past Roy Garland's table she wondered why was Jamie's aunt still sitting there.

"I'm sure by the time Aunt Eileen is finished with the man she'll have all of his family secrets." Jamie looked down at the next order.

"It's just that he's so… touchy."

The double doors swung open and Donna hurried in. "Anyone else wondering what your aunt is doing with the ass patting Councilman Garland?"

Frowning, Jamie looked from one waitress to the other. "Wait a minute. Are we talking about the same man? On the tail end of middle age, slightly rotund, comb-over to hide the bald spot, always smiling?"

Like a matched set, Abbie and Donna nodded.

"He's from a different era." Abbie shrugged. "According to the sisters, his nickname in high school was octopus hands."

"Wait a minute. How touchy is touchy?"

"It's not that bad. As long as Old Octopus Hands doesn't take me out on a date, I have nothing to worry about."

"Has he asked you?"

The growing alarm on Jamie's face was almost amusing. Abbie had to strain to keep a straight face. "Only in a teasing way. You know, *run away with me and you'll never work another day in your life* kind of thing. We waitresses get that all the time."

"Uh huh." Jamie's grip on the paper in his hands tightened.

"Whatever." Abbie turned on her heel.

"Wait."

She pivoted around. "What?"

"Grace has been working late a lot with the council members. You don't think he… you know?"

This time Abbie laughed out right. "No, I don't. The guy may have itchy fingers, but I've never heard him disrespect a married woman, ever."

"So you agree he's being disrespectful."

"Well of course I do. It's not your backside he likes to pat. I'm just saying we cut the old goat a little slack around here and keep a wide berth and everybody's happy."

"Yeah well, I think it may be time for the Farradays to have a little chat with his honor Mr. Councilman."

"That's fine with me, but I suggest you wait until after all the permits have been issued."

Jamie slid a frying pan onto the burner, grumbling something about doing it but not liking it.

One of the double doors swung open, stopping Abbie in her tracks.

Standing under the doorway, his aunt Eileen held the door with one hand and flashed a thumbs up with the other, and whispered, "Sorry to barge in, but I wanted to let you know we've got this covered."

"Oh that's wonderful." Abbie leaned forward to hug Eileen and noticed Roy walking toward the kitchen. "We have company," she whispered.

Aunt Eileen looked over her shoulder. Spotting the councilman, she straightened and plastered on a huge smile.

"Roy?"

Giving a brief nod to Jamie in the back, the man smiled at Eileen. "You are sure we are all set for dinner?"

"Absolutely, consider it a date."

Grinning with an unusual amount of boyish charm she never would've expected to come from the old goat, the man smiled up at Jamie and Abbie, then wiggling his fingers, waved goodbye to Eileen. Abbie would've bet a month's wages the guy was going to dance down the sidewalk as soon as the front door closed behind him.

"What have you done?" Jamie turned off the stove and walked around to where his aunt and Abbie stood.

"Don't look so horrified. I found out what he wants and now he'll get it."

Abbie swallowed what little saliva was left in her mouth. "You're going on a dinner date with the Roy Garland?"

"Of course not." Shaking her head, Aunt Eileen turned halfway and pushed the door open to the restaurant. "Sally May is."

"Sally May agreed to go to dinner with him?" Abbie and Jamie echoed.

Aunt Eileen's smile grew. "No, but she will."

Before Abbie could say another word, the door swung loudly behind his aunt. She turned to face Jamie.

His jaw slightly open, his eyes still on the swinging door, he mumbled, "We've created a monster."

• • • •

"Well," Jamie turned back to the cooktop. "One thing is for sure, we can't let Sally May go on a dinner date with Mr. Octopus just so that the Farradays can open a pub."

Donna came hurrying in. "Bunch of teams just came in. Get ready to do a lot a hamburgers and fries." She slapped an order down in front of Jamie and turned, hurrying back out the door.

"I'd better get back to work. We'll figure something out." Abbie followed behind the other waitress.

All he wanted to know was how did everything get so crazy. A simple deal. A simple plan. An Irish pub. Now his aunt was negotiating dinner dates with a dirty old man, vegetable gardens with sourpuss temperance ladies, and he didn't dare consider what she might come up with next.

CHAPTER FOURTEEN

"I definitely can see the charm in Tuckers Bluff. Oh man." Sitting on a counter stool, Dave slurped a taste of Irish Stew from a spoon. "This is amazing."

"Let me." His wife pilfered the spoon and swallowed the last bit of broth. "Oh, amazing doesn't cut it."

Jamie couldn't stop from smiling. It had only taken him four batches to get it right.

"Told you." Abbie leaned her elbow on the counter. Typical for a Sunday afternoon, the restaurant had been closed for over an hour. She, Jamie, and his friends from Dallas had been laughing, and exchanging stories, and experimenting with recipes.

"I never said I doubted you." Leaning over, about to plant a delighted kiss on her lips, Jamie realized in the nick of time how inappropriate that would be and diverted to a quick peck on her forehead. "I would have done this recipe from now till doomsday and not recognized that my hands and my great grandmother's hands are not the same size."

Dave's wife swallowed another taste. "I don't understand?"

"The recipe," Jamie poured a bowl for each of them, "was passed down from woman to woman in my mom's family and it went mostly a pinch of this and a handful of that."

"Ah," Dave nodded.

"Right. My hands are bigger than any of my maternal ancestors." He waved a thumb at Abbie. "She figured it out."

Abbie shrugged, taking a quick taste of the stew. "I remembered reading that somewhere about one of the cookie companies. Don't remember which one, but it struck me that her problem copying her grandmother's recipe could have been your problem."

"So we used Abbie's hands." Jamie resisted the urge once again to lean over and kiss her. Instead he took a step back. Anything to keep his mind on the food. "I'm also thinking that Abbie's pinch and handful are closer to my great grandmother's because even mom's stew doesn't turn out this good."

Dave's wife Beverly blew on a spoon. "I wish we were going to be around long enough to try out everything on your menu."

"Me too," Dave added.

The overhead bell on the café door jingled. Even though they were no longer open for business, they hadn't bothered to lock the door. Something that both surprised and delighted him. After Abbie had rehashed all the dark memories, he was glad to see that she didn't still feel jittery. At least not enough to have been conscientious about the café door.

"Hello," two female voices sang.

Sissy, a tall willowy redhead led the way. "Meg said we'd find you here."

"Hello," Beverly said. "Nice to see you again."

"Then you've met?" Abbie asked.

Dave and his wife nodded.

"Oh, yes," Sissy answered. "They were in the shop yesterday with Meg and Eileen for a little while. Told us about the new baby. Such sweet pictures."

"That's one of the nice things about this newfangled electronic world," Sissy chimed in. "So many lovely photos at your fingertips on a cell phone."

"Well," Sister, the shorter of the two women who still wore her platinum blonde hair as wide as it was high, reached into her purse. "After we spoke yesterday, I knew we had at least one more of the hand carved rattles."

"The other one belongs to Ethan's little girl now, but the man who carved it had made a spare and brought it into us not that long ago," Sissy explained.

"I don't know how we'd forgotten about it." Sister produced a lovely handcrafted baby rattle.

"Oh my," Beverly's eyes widened. "That's just lovely. And so light."

Sissy smiled beside her sister. "The only thing the maker asked of us is that it be given to a special baby."

"That's right," Sister nodded. "While we haven't met your little bundle, we can tell from our visit with you yesterday that the craftsman would be happy."

Beverly looked up, passing the rattle to her husband. "How much does he want for it?"

"Oh, he doesn't want money for it," Sister said quickly.

"But so much work," Dave fingered the lovely item. "Surely—"

Sissy cut him off with the wave of a hand. "We'd all be mighty pleased if you'd accept it."

Dave and his wife looked to Jamie.

He nodded. "That's the way things are done around here."

"Yes," Dave mumbled, handing the rattle back to his wife. The two stared at each other long and hard. Jamie recognized the scene before him as one he'd seen many times in his own household between his mom and dad and often at the ranch between his Uncle Sean and Aunt Eileen. The silent conversation of a couple who didn't need words to communicate. Then Dave raised one brow, Beverly smiled and nodded, and Jamie knew they'd come to an agreement.

Beverly turned and smiled at the sisters then settled her gaze on Jamie. "Meg took me to her neighbor's house up the block. It's just lovely and will be going up for sale soon. The family has outgrown it."

"Yes," Sissy nodded. "That would be Ken and Elizabeth Ashridge. Just had their fourth baby, well, fourth and fifth."

"Such a blessing to have twins," Sister added. "Even if it was a bit of a surprise."

"Surprise?" Jamison thought today's world of 3D sonograms and DNA testing that parents knew everything about their baby short of its IQ.

"Apparently one baby kept hiding behind the other," Abbie explained to him

Sister nodded. "They're building a house not too far from Brooks and Toni's."

"We drove by that as well yesterday," Beverly continued. "The Ashridges' old house would be perfect for a growing family."

"What my wife is taking the long road to say is, we'd like very much to raise our family in Tuckers Bluff."

"Yes," Jamie cheered, practically leaping over the counter, pulling his friend into back slapping hug before turning to embrace the man's wife. "Welcome to Tuckers Bluff."

"Our first new residents, and new jobs thanks to O'Fearadaigh's," Abbie beamed. "We'll see what the town council says about that."

The councilman. One problem solved and another one at his feet. He had no choice, he would have to sit down with Force Eileen for a nice long chat. Then all he had to do was figure out how to break the anticipated date without ticking off one too friendly councilman.

• • • •

"Okay, ice cream and crème de almond tastes way too good to be saddled with a name like Pink Squirrel." After Dave and his wife had returned to the B&B, Abbie and Jamie worked on the liquor choices for the cook-off event. She took another sip of the concoction in front of her. This sucker was fantastic. "I've heard of some crazy named drinks, but why would anyone name something so tasty after a laxative colored rodent?"

"Mom didn't say." Jamie rinsed out the blender. "All she told me was that my grandmother Farraday had one every afternoon before dinner. If it's good enough for my Irish Granny, the name is good enough for O'Fearadaigh's. So this is a definite for serving the cook-off day?"

Abbie shrugged. "I'm torn between how delicious the thing is and serving something that looks so much like a strawberry milkshake."

Frowning down at the empty blender, Jamie huffed. "I hadn't thought about that. Maybe we should cross this one off the list.

"You can if you want, but I do admit this sucker is fantastic."

Smiling, Jamie shook his head. "So yes or no?"

"It's your cook-off."

"And," his heated gaze bore into her, "I'm asking your opinion."

"Oh." *Get a grip Abbie*. "Well," she sucked in a deep calming breath, "yes. After all we'll be serving beer and wine so it will be obvious that the bar end of the café is not for children."

His grin took over his face. "There we go. Pink Squirrels it is."

Abbie took another sip. "They really are delicious."

"Yeah, well, they pack a wallop if you drink 'em like milk shakes."

"Noted." Abbie saluted him. Not sure why since he wasn't a Marine like Frank or Ethan.

"These are the beers." From under the counter, Jamie hefted a large carton onto the top and, one by one, pulled out different beers. "Not all are Dave's, but I thought we'd pick maybe three or four as a sampling beside the standard tap offerings."

"Do you think three or four is enough?"

Jamie's brow shot high on his forehead. "Don't you?"

"Nope." Abbie shook her head. "You should out do Hemingway's in all things. Let the town know their options."

"Then let's choose the ones."

It was fun watching him working in his element. Unlike the first day in the kitchen where he needed some getting used to, here behind the counter, even though it wasn't set up like a real bar, Jamie opened and poured the beers with just the right amount of froth every time.

By the fifth sample, Abbie decided they should have asked someone else to do the tasting. Not a true beer fan, they were all beginning to taste the same. "I still think my favorites were the first two, though I'm not sure if it's because they were that much better or now they're all blending together."

"The first two were lighter. The last one was a dark ale, not everyone likes the darker brew."

"I've heard that." Abbie lifted her chin, pointing at the next carton. "What's that?"

"These are the wines from Brady's." He set a bottle in front of her.

Her gaze followed his movements as he removed each bottle from the box. "Ooh, they do a Pinot Grigio. I like that."

"They do a Pinot Noir too. And of course a Cabernet." He lifted one of the bottles with the white label. "And recently they've won an award for this Chardonnay."

"So four standards?" The bell over the front door announced a visitor. "You expecting anyone?"

At the same time Jamie shook his head, much to Abbie's surprise, Mabel Berkner waltzed into the café. "Your aunt mentioned at church this morning that you two would be working here this afternoon."

"I was just showing Abbie the wines from Brady's." Jamie set the bottle down and waved Mabel inside. "Take a seat."

"Thank you." Mable made herself comfortable on the stool in front of Jamie. "You'll do well with Brady's. They use French oak for their Pinot Noir and Chardonnay."

One eyebrow cocked high with surprise, Jamie shot a sideways glance at Abbie. She hadn't expected the woman to know anything about wines either.

"Less vanillin from the wood," Mabel continued. "Makes a huge difference in the flavor over time."

"Would you like a glass?" Jamie offered.

"No thanks, I have errands to run. Have a bunch of mason jars I want to give to Eileen. Canning is not for me."

"I'd be happy to take them home tonight if you want to leave them here," Jamie offered.

"Thanks, but that's not why I'm here. It's a lovely day for a ride out to the ranch. The reason I'm here is your aunt came to talk to me the other day. She and Sally. They made some good points. I'm getting on in years."

"Like a good wine," Jamie smiled.

Mabel laughed. "At least you didn't compare me to cheese."

The Farraday smile was in full force and judging by the way Mabel blushed, it still had an impact even among the senior citizens.

"As I was saying, I've put up a good long fight to keep this county dry but it's time for you younger folks to decide what you want for this town. This county."

"All we want," Jamie said, "is what's best for everybody."

"And that brings me to the next point. Your aunt is right. The Farraday's and the Berkner's have cared about this town for long before any of us were born." She waved her arm at the bottles on the counter. "Serve Brady's wine, bring in the new beer maker to town with his family, and I'm guessing you'll be sourcing local foods and vegetables."

Jamie nodded. "That's the plan. We even have a few surprises when it comes to baked goods."

"Is that why your aunt Eileen wants a new kitchen?"

"She wants a new kitchen?" he asked.

"Eileen may have said something about that."

"If she does want the new kitchen, it's not for baking. That will be Toni's domain."

Mabel's expression lifted. "Oh, she does bake a good cake."

"Yes, that too."

"Well that makes me feel even better about my decision." Mabel glanced from Jamie to Abbie and back. "You have my full support on getting the liquor license for the pub. I see no reason to bring an out-of-state company into town and have them shipping all their profits away from Tuckers Bluff."

Anyone would think the pub was hers the way Abbie's heart did an Irish jig at Mabel's endorsement.

"That's great news." Jamie flew around the counter and practically lifted Mabel out of her seat into a huge hug.

Flustered, when he let go of her the woman brushed away non-existent wrinkles. "Yes. Well. It's the neighborly thing to do."

"Yes," Abbie agreed. "Very neighborly.

The over-door bell sounded again.

"Apparently we do better business when we're closed than when we're open," Jamie teased.

"Seems so." Abbie kept her eyes on the door, surprised to see Ian coming through.

"What brings you by, little brother? Aunt Eileen know you've gone AWOL?"

Mabel's eyes rounded and Abbie almost spit with laughter. After all, Ian was as big as Jamison. Two men cut from the same cloth. Either would have been very intimidating in a dark alley, together they could scare off an entire enemy battalion.

"Just came from there. On my way out to the old Peterson Trail." Ian took a seat beside Mabel." Spotted the lights on in here and since I have a few minutes to spare thought I'd stop in a second."

Jamie frowned. "Something wrong?"

"Actually, quite the opposite." Ian waved a finger at the wine and the beer. "Seems the new referendum is working in the county much the way the end of prohibition worked against the bootleggers a century ago. Word is the main moonshiner who's been evading the law since forever is retiring."

Smiling broadly, Jamie lifted a high five to Abbie, Mabel and then his brother, "This calls for a celebratory drink."

"I'm on the clock." Ian waved away the proffered beer bottle. "Before you throw a party, rumor also has it that there's going to be one last major delivery of white lightning today. State police and the Sherriff's department have brought in all available manpower to cover every back road and trail possible."

"Why such a big push if they're retiring?" Abbie asked.

"From West Texas, maybe, but there's always a chance

someone in the chain will just move on to be someone else's headache."

"Unless you stop them." Abbie should have realized that.

"Then go get 'em, bro." Jamie went for another round of high fives, stopping short at Mabel's dour expression.

Mabel moved to stand. "I've said my piece, I'd better be moving on." She straightened her back and faced Jamie. "You let me know if there's anything I can do besides talk the ears off the town council."

"I will." Jamie nodded. "And thank you."

Mabel hurried out the door, rummaging through her purse, producing both her keys and phone by the time she'd reached the door.

"Did I hear correctly?" Ian eyed his brother. "Have you converted the enemy?"

"Looks that way."

Abbie reached for a rag and wiped the counter. "What surprises me almost as much, is her making an effort at being friends with your aunt. That I know of, that woman has never been friends with anyone."

"Stranger things have happened." Jamie shrugged. "But I think she'll be surprised to find the last thing Aunt Eileen's going to want is more mason jars."

"Mason jars?" Ian asked.

"Yeah, Mabel doesn't want to do canning anymore so she's donating her leftover mason jars to Aunt Eileen. A peace offering, I suspect."

"Peace offering," Ian muttered, getting up and moving to the window. His gaze on Mabel as she turned the engine and raced away from the diner. He pivoted around to face his brother. "Doesn't she have a nephew?"

"Yeah," Abbie nodded, "But he and his mom moved away from town a long time ago. Every once in a while he'll visit though."

"Wonder what he drives?" Ian seemed to be more thinking

aloud than asking questions.

"Don't know but it roars like a hungry lion when he starts the engine," Abbie laughed.

Ian returned his gaze to the window and shook his head. “Sometimes this business makes us too cynical. For a second there I actually considered that nice old lady could be our bootlegger."

Jamie barked with laughter. “Okay, that's a stretch. I mean...”

“Yeah.” Ian smiled. “I’ve got to get a move on. If all goes well you’ll be reading about this in the papers.”

“Good luck,” Abbie called after him. For as long as she’d lived in Tuckers Bluff she’d known about the local moonshine operation, but somehow she thought it rather unfair that right when the bootlegger decides to retire the law would make such a big push to stop them. “I know I shouldn’t, but I feel kind of sorry for them.”

“What do you mean?” Jamie sidled next to her.

“I don’t know. I guess a law breaker is a law breaker. But wouldn’t it be something if Ian’s instincts were right and teetotaling Mabel is our mastermind bootlegger?” Not till she’d spun around in place and bumped into Jamie’s chest did she realize just how close he’d been standing to her.

“Yes,” he agreed softly, his gaze latching onto hers, his hands falling gently to her sides.

Her breath trapped under her beating heart, Abbie managed to nod and mumble, “Uh huh” seconds before Jamie’s mouth descended on hers. Soft, sweet, and gentle, it was the most tender kiss she’d ever received. Before she could move her arms or inch closer, he pulled away.

Letting his forehead lean lightly against hers, his warm breath blew against her face. “I shouldn’t have done that.”

Why not, she wanted to say. But nothing came out.

“What are the chances of me being run out of town on a rail if I were to,” he sucked in a deep breath but didn’t move, “do that again?”

Did he really just ask if he could kiss her again? Because if she'd had any say in the matter they wouldn't have stopped the first time.

"I'm sorry," he whispered, retracting a step.

She realized she hadn't voiced her thoughts, pushing him away with her silence.

"If I promise," he continued, "never to drink another Pink Squirrel can you forgive me?"

Was that it? Was it the drink that had driven him kiss her? Ludicrous, a man his size could handle mixing drinks.

Jamie inched further away, his expression shifting from playfully apologetic to dripping with concern. Rubbing his hand along the back of his neck, he sucked in a long breath and leveled his gaze with here. "Please tell me I haven't totally botched our friendship."

Friendship? She'd been kissed many times by many people. On the cheek, on the forehead, even a peck here or there on the lips and none had ever felt anything like the too brief feel of his mouth on hers. If that kiss was in the name of friendship, her name was Scarlett O'Hara.

"Abbie," he said softly.

She might be shooting herself in the proverbial foot. Or perhaps hammering the final nail in the coffin of friendship, but if it meant moving onto better things, that was a chance she was willing to take.

"Sometimes," she moved into his personal space, "words are highly over-rated."

CHAPTER FIFTEEN

If Jamie had died and gone to heaven, that was perfectly all right with him. Abbie molded against him and every fiber of his being went on high alert. Had anyone ever felt so perfectly right in his arms before?

A soft cough rumbled in the distance, followed by a second louder cough, sending Abbie springing backward.

"Didn't mean to interrupt." Frank stood leaning heavily to one side, a large black orthopedic boot on his bad leg, the intensity of his gaze belying his statement. "I've been sprung."

"Frank," Abbie squealed hurrying to his side. "Sprung or flew the coup?"

"Would I lie to you?"

"Yes," she deadpanned, both hands fisted on her hips. "If you thought it was for my own good."

The stern expression on Frank's face gave way to a smothered chuckle. "Touché, but in this case I have been promoted to this boot." Frank pointed down to the bulky boot on his bad leg.

"And a lovely boot it is," Abbie smiled

"No one could complain about the Farraday hospitality, but I am ready to sleep in my own bed again."

Brooks popped inside. "No matter what he says, the boot is not a ticket to spend all day standing in the kitchen."

Jamie was pretty sure he heard Frank snarl.

"Short spurts only," Brooks admonished.

Abbie swiveled around to face Brooks. "What do you mean by spurts?"

"Twenty minutes or so. Thirty tops. Then he needs to put it up for a bit." Brooks stared pointedly at Frank giving Jamie the impression this was an old argument.

"I can help," Frank insisted.

"Not in the kitchen," Brooks countered. "Not yet."

Frank rolled his eyes. "Bossiness sure runs in the family."

"Thank you." Brooks tossed him a big grin and turned to Abbie. "I'm taking him home now. If he tries to come back as anything more than a customer for another week, you let me know."

"You got it," Abbie said.

"At least let me see what your kin has done to my kitchen."

Brooks looked down at his watch. "Okay, but let's make it quick. Toni and the baby are waiting for me in the car."

"Why don't you leave Frank here?" Jamie suggested. "I can give him a ride home later."

Brooks studied his cousin then turned to Frank. The official café cook nodded and Brooks faced Jamie. "Guess he's all yours. Good luck keeping him off his feet."

"Don't you worry about that," Abbie assured Brooks. "I may not be a Marine, but I've worked for one long enough to know how it's done."

Frank muffled a groan.

"We've got Irish Stew and corned beef and cabbage on the stove. Want me to warm up a taste before you make inspection?"

"Wouldn't mind a taste. Or a look at this new menu."

"It's for the cook-off next week." Jamie put a placemat in front of Frank.

"That's what I heard."

"Oh," Abbie paused at the kitchen doors, "you should try the sauce for dipping French fries. Sounds disgusting when you hear it's mayonnaise based, but it tastes really good."

"Mayonnaise?" Frank's lips curled downward.

"Like she said," Jamie pointed over his shoulder at Abbie's disappearing back, "tastes good."

Frank nodded, watching the doors wobble closed. When they were firmly shut, he settled his gaze on Jamie. "How long has this been going on?"

"This?" Jamie hoped this was referring to something benign like the license competition.

"Don't be obtuse. I don't have long before she comes back. That was one hell of a liplock."

Jamie couldn't stop the corners of his lips from turning up at the memory. It really was. The kiss was also none of Frank's business. "And your point?"

"That girl matters to me. A great deal." Frank must have seen the questions in Jamie's eyes because he quickly continued, "She may not be my daughter by bloodline, but she is in every other way that counts. We go back a long time. Been through more than most folks."

"I know."

His bushy brows shot up. "She told you?"

Jamie nodded.

"Everything?"

"About that lunatic and the knife? Yes."

"I see." Frank began twirling the spoon Jamie had set out for him.

Jamie resisted the urge to fidget, find something else to do. Frank was sizing him up and he knew it. For some inexplicable reason, Jamie really wanted to pass muster.

"You care for her."

It wasn't a question but Jamie nodded anyhow. "Yes, sir."

"A lot."

He didn't have to think on that. He'd already figured that one out for himself. "Yes, sir."

"Enough to risk your life for her?"

Without blinking, Jamie nodded. "I'd kill for her."

"So would I." Frank set the spoon down. "You're in love with her?"

"Ye—" Jamie stopped mid-sentence. The words processing more clearly. Not the questions, but his reply. A knee jerk reaction to what had been all affirmative statements, he had to pause. Turning over the last few weeks in his mind, the way his heart rate changed when she was near, the way her smile made him want to smile, the way her laugh made him forget his troubles, the fierce urge to keep her safe that took over at the slightest break in routine.

The doors swung open and Abbie carried in two dishes, barely breaking stride to pause and wink at him.

His stomach did a somersault and smiling wide enough to feel his face crack, he winked back at her, then caught a glimpse of the grumpy Marine nodding at him. Son of a…. How about that. He was most definitely head over boot heels in love with his temporary boss.

• • • •

"Sounds like you've got everything figured out." Frank climbed into the passenger seat of Jamie's truck.

"Considering how fast this whole thing had to come together, I don't think we've forgotten anything." Since she would be the first to be dropped off tonight, Abbie opted for the back seat. Strapping herself in, she took in the way Frank and Jamie seemed to be sending coded messages with only a glance. At first she thought Frank was annoyed with Jamie. Despite the few good words, okay maybe not good, but if Frank didn't criticize then that was the same as a compliment and he had not criticized a single thing Jamie had done in the kitchen. Yet, most of the time Frank seemed to be censuring Jamie. Maybe warning him off. She couldn't put her finger on it. Only when she noticed Jamie occasionally dip his chin or suck in a deep breath did she realize the men were actually communicating. By the time she left the café she was waiting for one of them to pee along the walk and mark his territory.

"Mighty nice of Meg to step in and help, I mean seeing she has her own business to run," Frank said.

"If Shannon, Donna and I can handle it on our own, then Meg can fill in somewhere else, but we all discussed it and felt that having four waitresses on board for the constant movement would be best."

"You really think that many folks are going to be coming by?" Frank asked.

"Chase has had a notice up at the feed store and the other merchants have also. Lots of folks who only come into town once a month for shopping or services have promised to come by."

"Lots is subjective." Frank looked at Abbie over his shoulder. "I hadn't expected you to be such a big part of this."

"It's been fun. More fun than I would have thought."

"I see you're not worried anymore?"

"Nope. I've been convinced." Abbie flashed her cook and friend a big toothy grin. The one that always made him shake his head and smile. Only this time all she got was the head shake. Something was definitely bothering Frank and Abbie didn't think it had anything to do with his foot.

A few feet before Abbie's house, a small fluffy flash blew across the street and Jamie slammed on the brakes.

"Are you trying to break the rest of me?" Frank barked.

"Did you see that?" Jamie asked.

Frank's grimace deepened. "See what?"

"There," Abbie shouted, pointing to the puppy sitting quietly on the curb across the street.

"You two wait here a minute, let me get him. Maybe we'll find out once and for all who that pup belongs to," Jamie said.

"I can help." Abbie reached for the handle but Jamie waved her off.

"He seems to like me. This shouldn't take but a second."

Nodding, Abbie watched him strut across the street. Heavens, that man knew how to walk.

"You like him."

The sound of Frank's voice dragged her attention away from the man she'd practically been drooling over. "He's a nice guy. All the Farradays are."

"Yeah, but you don't look at all the Farradays the way you

look at him."

"Oh, and how is that?"

"Like he was the last ice scream sundae on the planet and the only one with extra whipped cream."

Was she really that easy to read? Did the whole town think she looked at Jamie that way? "I do not." *Way to go, big girl.* She might as well throw herself on the floor and stomp her feet like a three year old.

This time, Frank smiled. "Don't you worry. No one else knows you as well as I do. I just can't make up my mind if you falling in love with a Farraday is a good thing or not."

"Falling in love." She glanced out the window at Jamie on the ground, holding the puppy in his arms and scratching his ears. Her heart swelled and her stomach took a nose dive. She almost couldn't breathe. Was this what falling in love felt like? The puppy licked Jamie's face, making him laugh and her heart soared. Who was she kidding? She was definitely head over high heels in love with that man. And wouldn't it be nice if he were the first to know it, not half the town. "Who said anything about falling in love?"

Frank laughed a little harder. "Don't you two make the pair? Here comes the Irish cowboy now. With that damn dog. Should have known the minute that blasted pup cozied up to the man."

The opposite back door opened and Jamie set the tail-wagging pup inside. "After I get Frank home I'll take this little guy to Adam. See if we can't find out who he belongs to." No sooner had the words left his mouth than the little guy gave his hand a long lick and hopping onto the floorboards, took a leap out of the truck and bolted before Jamie could stop him. "Blast."

Frank huffed under his breath. "He'll be back. I'd start house hunting if I were you."

Her mind scrolled forward to visions of a house, a dog, and Jamie at her side. Now wouldn't that be one hell of a dream come true?

CHAPTER SIXTEEN

Since closing down early Friday night, the entire kitchen of the café had been scrubbed to within an inch of its stainless-steel life. Along with the cleaning crew that had come through and scoured every nook and cranny of the cafe, just about every Farraday sibling from one side of the family or the other had come by to do their share.

Little was left to be done this morning other than last minute decorations and setting up the parking lot for overflow.

Jamie scanned the banners draped from the ceilings. Too excited and anxious to sleep, at four this morning he'd given up on any pretense of resting and gotten out of bed. By six he was on his way to the café. He shouldn't have been that surprised to have Abbie walking in the door only a few minutes after him.

Together they'd hung the *Welcome to a Taste of Tuckers Bluff* banner, sorted the paper goods and double and triple checked the to-do list in preparation for Crocker arrival.

Arms carrying a bundle of plastic checkered tablecloths, Abbie came out from the storage room. The last few days he'd felt like a kid in high school. Anxious, excited and nervous at something as simple as a few seconds to hold Abbie's hand, or to share a barely there peck on the lips. With so much hanging on today, they'd not really discussed the kiss on her porch. Somehow he knew once the pub and license business was all settled, they'd have plenty of time to do a lot more than just talk about that kiss. And he, for one, was looking dang forward to it.

She sidled up beside him. "The kids did a great job."

"Better than great." The high school art department had come through with colorful and creative signage for everything from the menu cards to the large O'Fearadaigh's banner, his personal favorite. He was going to have to find a permanent home for it when the pub opened. *If* the pub opened.

The front door blew open at the same time Sally May's voice boomed across the threshold. "You did what?" The clearly annoyed woman spun around, glaring at his aunt.

"Uh oh." Abbie lowered her voice, "Either your aunt has joined the French Foreign Legion, or I'm guessing this is the first Sally May has heard about her plans with the councilman."

Eileen rolled her eyes at Sally May and blew out a sigh. "Oh, don't get your panties in a wad. I didn't promise you'd marry the man, just join him for dinner."

"Since when do you make my dinner dates for me?"

"I can go you one better. When was the last time you went on a dinner date at all?"

Sally May grunted and Jamie almost lost it when she spun around and leaning forward, stuck her tongue out at his aunt like a little kid before storming in his direction, calling over her shoulder, "I'm not going on a date with that old coot."

"He's younger than you, and it's not a date, it's dinner."

"Tahmaytoe, tahmahtoe." Sally May waved a jerky arm at her friend, stomping closer to the counters where Jamie and Abbie stood. "I am not going anywhere with that man."

Aunt Eileen quickened her pace to keep up with the woman several inches taller than her. "Not even O'Fearadaigh's?"

That was enough to have Sally May stop short and whirl around. "What are you talking about?"

"Do I look like a senile ditz?"

Sally May raised a brow but didn't respond.

"Never mind. I figured it was too hard and not enough time to uncover who on the council was really for or against us *and* convince them why our pub would be good for this town. Then it hit me talking to Meg earlier in the week. Why not let him convince everyone for us? If he wants that dinner with you badly enough, he'll move heaven and earth to get the council to see more clearly."

Shoulders stiff with fury deflated slowly as Sally May blew out a steady breath. "As much as I hate to admit it, that's not a bad idea."

Holding back a chuckle, Jamie leaned into Abbie and mumbled through the side of his mouth, "Score one for Aunt Eileen."

"Certainly beats spying on them like a couple of bratty siblings." Abbie squeezed his arm then walked away, shaking her head.

Much like the responsibility he'd felt for Frank falling and hurting himself at the site of the future pub, he felt equally guilty for Sally May being used as a pawn in the pub's future. So much so that ever since they'd heard about the plans his aunt had made, he and Abbie had batted possibilities back and forth, from confronting the councilman, to insisting Aunt Eileen get Sally May out of it, to following after the councilman and Sally May on their date like a couple of nuisance little kids, and if the letch laid even one inappropriate finger on Sally May, Jamie was prepared to teach that man a lesson about respect and women that he should have learned in grade school.

Her argument with Sally May apparently behind them, at least for now, Aunt Eileen looked up at him. "When are the Hemingway's people arriving?"

"Any minute. The kitchen is ready to go. Dave is all set as well." Jamie waved his arm across the café. "I have a good feeling about all this."

His aunt looped her arm around his waist and leaned into him. "So do I. So do I."

• • • •

"Six Corned Beef samples, six Stew samples," Shannon called to Jamie behind the counter on the Farraday side of the kitchen and filling a tray, pivoted ninety degrees and hurried down to the Hemingway's side. "Two vegan burger samples, one eggplant

BLT."

It still boggled Jamie's mind that anyone wanted to sample an eggplant BLT. Of course he hadn't wrapped his mind around how anything without bacon could still be called a BLT.

"I'm here to replace you." Toni rushed straight to the rack of aprons on the rear wall. "Everything is hopping. Even with more tables in the parking lot the line is going around the corner. I think the whole dang county showed up. The shops all have their doors open and took down the no food or drink signs. Everyone is wandering up and down the street. The market is breaking up their frozen pop boxes and selling them on the sidewalk like an old-fashioned lemonade stand. I've never seen anything like this."

Moving at full speed and praying they didn't run out of food, Jaimie had never been so happy to come from a big Irish family that believed in cooking twice as much as needed. He was also overjoyed that every time his aunt shook her head and said not enough, he listened and bought more fixings than he ever expected to possibly serve. "I admit I could use the help."

"Not here to help. To replace." Toni tied the apron behind her. "The big wigs from Hemingway's are out there schmoozing so you should be too. Not that all the Farradays aren't doing a fine job of it, but you're the face of O'Fearadaigh's."

It had been all he could do to keep up with the demand. He couldn't in good conscious leave Toni on her own in the kitchen.

"What's the hold up?" Becky came rushing into the kitchen, Donna on her heels.

Donna hurried past Becky. "Adam and Connor are setting up a tent outside that the sisters donated. Should have done it hours ago. I need you to load me up or we'll never get everyone fed."

"I think I see the problem." Becky scurried over to the aprons and grabbed one. "I'll help Toni," she looked at Jamie, "you get your derriere outside and do your thing, and tell Catherine to come inside and grab an apron. Connor can keep an eye on Stacey."

"Or Ethan. He's on Brittany duty. Stacey can probably help him. I love the guy but he woefully underestimates how fast a toddler can run when she knows you're not looking."

Dorothy appeared in the doorway, half in and half out. "Need more hands?"

"Yeah." Toni waved at the deck shelf. "Help Donna carry out samples. They're setting up a station outside."

"Yes, ma'am." Dorothy saluted and not bothering with an apron, loaded an empty tray. "This is so exciting."

The women hurried about like an army of well-organized ants. The Hemmingway staff watched, a glazed look in their eyes. They were staying busy, but not nearly as harried as Jamie and the girls were. Without any help from the family, Hemingway's' staff easily spared a pair of hands to transport their samples to the new outdoor set up. As crazy as the day was, this was why he wanted so badly to move home. Family was more than blood, it was everything.

"Okay." Abbie came into the kitchen, momentarily startled by the extra people. Apparently she hadn't been privy to the onslaught of help. "Uh, Dave wants you to pop outside to the bar set up when you can."

"Anything wrong?" Everything was going so well, something was bound to get messed up. When it did he merely hoped whatever it was would be easily fixable. And fast.

She shook her head. "Quite the contrary. The Pink Squirrels are a hit. On the other hand, the crazy drink Hemingway's is serving that lights up like a cherries jubilee is doing a great job of entertaining the children but they're having a hard time convincing the adults to drink them. They're having the same problem with the drink poured over dry ice."

Where had they come up with such a crazy idea? Jamie wasn't surprised the showy drinks weren't going over with as much enthusiasm as Crocker and Hemingway's had most likely expected. Country folks like simple. Even when they gussied up, they still liked simple.

"Go." Toni shooed him away. "We've got this."

"Yeah. Go," Becky echoed.

Curiosity had been getting the better of him for hours now. “Okay. If you need anything, someone whistle for me.”

“Got it,” Becky answered, waving him away again.

By the time Jamie made it within view of the large picture frame windows, his jaw almost hit the floor. Filled with people, some on line, some milling about, the sidewalk resembled a scene from a big city like New York or San Francisco. The difference—all these people were smiling. “Do you think it’s just the free food?”

“It’s not free,” Abbie said, her eyes on the same people happily meandering outside, and laughing and gabbing inside.

“When did that happen?” This was supposed to be on their dime.

“This morning. When the crowds lined up all through town before we opened, the council feared a mob scene might erupt over who knows what. Hemingway’s big shots along with your dad and Uncle Sean argued that wasn’t the intent, but since price had not been mentioned in any of the advertising or invitations, they lost the argument. Everyone did, however, agree that the proceeds would go to the hospital.”

Nodding, Jamie looked around. “Well, the people don’t seem upset by it.”

“Why should they? It’s all for a good cause, and they’re having the time of their life.” Abbie smiled up at him. “It’s all because of you.”

The way her eyes twinkled up at him made everything else in the world slip away. Almost. If they weren’t in a public place in the middle of one of the most important days of his life, he would have ignored everyone around him and pulled her in for one of those mind blowing kisses he’d been anticipating after this all was behind them. He’d almost leaned in regardless when the sounds of “Danny Boy” came blasting in from the street. “What’s that?”

Abbie chuckled. “I think someone gave your mom and your aunt a microphone.”

“Oh, brother.” At least they could both carry a tune.

Outside a crowd had gathered around his mom and aunt. The townsfolk were loving it. And so was his family. His aunt looked absolutely radiant, reminding him of what his cousins had said about photos of her singing. The way she held the mic, moved it closer or farther away from her mouth depending on the notes, the way her free arm moved. It wouldn't be hard to believe she'd been a professional singer once upon a time.

By the time he made it out the front door, Catherine hurried past him, calling out to make sure Ethan kept on eye on both kids.

"Will do," he answered. A couple of years ago his mom and aunt were singing the 'no grandchildren blues' and now there were little ones everywhere. Yep, nothing like family.

"There you are." Dave grinned up at him from behind the makeshift bar. "Are you sure we're in the middle of nowhere West Texas?"

Jamie had to laugh. "If you see anyone in red ruby slippers carrying a small dog, the answer is no, I'm not sure of anything."

Dave cracked up laughing and his wife elbowed him. "Laugh later, serve now."

"Yes, ma'am." Dave nodded, handing a customer two of his blonde beers.

"Do we have a favorite?" Jamie asked.

"Not really," Dave shrugged, "but we are keeping pace with the name brands. That's pretty good."

"Great. Exactly what I wanted to hear."

"The surprising thing is we're going through a good amount of stout."

That made Jamie laugh. You can take a family out of Ireland, but you can't take the Irish out of the family and they had plenty of Irish families in the county.

"Oh no," an alarmed voice sounded to Jamie's right.

Two large dogs galloped across the open expanse of the back end of the parking lot. Already taking off in that direction, he did a quick scan of the surroundings. At a fast glance he came to two conclusions, the animals were either after the newly set up tent with samples and Ethan slicing a large slab of corned beef, or the trio of little girls playing off to side. He hoped to high heaven it was the beef.

Kicking it into high gear, Jamie was within feet of the children when a crash boomed to one side of him. The one dog had veered off in the opposite direction and now was snarling at a puppy dragging a plate-filled checkered table cloth he'd successfully tugged off the table of guests. If Jamie wasn't mistaken, it was *the* puppy.

The other big dog vaulted in mid-air about to pounce on... another puppy? This one—who also looked a heck of a lot like *the* puppy—had his sights set on Ethan, or the corned beef or...the girls. Whichever, it wasn't the puppy that scared Jamie, it was the massive animal bounding towards them all.

From across the lot, Adam whistled and shouted, "Heads up."

His gaze moving from the growling dog across the way to Jamie coming upon him at full speed, alarm took over Ethan's face. Putting down the meat and the utensils, he turned scanning his surroundings, immediately spotting Brittany and his niece Stacey running in circles away from a puppy. A third puppy. *How the hell many dogs were there?*

The large gray dog landed with a thud less than a foot in front little Brittany and Jamie's heart lurched. Shoving off one foot, he dived for his niece, scooped her into his arms and cradling her tightly against her chest, curled into a ball. Concrete scraping the bare skin of his arms, he stopped with his back to the angry wolf.

"What the hell?" Ethan hollered.

Adam came flying at him. "You okay, man?"

A gentle touch patted his back, followed by a cold damp nose poking his neck.

"Can I have my daughter back?" Ethan's tone didn't carry any concern.

Turning slowly over, careful to protect his now crying niece in the event the dogs were still a threat, Jamie ignored the burning on his arms and took in the people staring at him as if he'd lost his mind.

"Come with Daddy, Princess." Ethan wrapped his hands around his little girl and hefted her into his arms. "It's all right. Uncle Jamie was just playing a silly game."

Adam pointed to the large wolf-looking animal sitting a couple of feet away, a puppy with a hunk of corned beef at its feet to one side and at the opposite side another puppy clenching an open ketchup bottle between its teeth wagged its tail. "I gather you've never met Gray?"

"Gray?" Jamie did a double take to make sure the gentle sitting animal was the same one he'd seen targeting the little girls. "That's someone's pet?"

"Not exactly," Ethan laughed.

The other dog that had been snarling at the tablecloth snatching pup came and sat beside the dog Adam called Gray. If Jamie didn't know better, he'd have sworn the two dogs were smiling. He also thought he saw them nod their heads at him. Pushing to his feet, he dusted off his jeans and smiled at the crowd that had gathered. "Sorry folks, please go enjoy your food."

He took one step forward to check if one of the puppies was *the* puppy when his foot skidded on a puddle of ketchup and before he could catch his balance, the third puppy dragging the plastic tablecloth behind him like superman's cape bumped against him, knocking his other leg out from under him. Like a Sunday morning cartoon strip his feet went up and his bottom went down. In slow motion he felt his head bounce on the concrete and the thought he should have kissed Abbie when he had the chance flashed through his mind seconds before closing his eyes and seeing black.

CHAPTER SEVENTEEN

Loaded down with a full tray, Abbie shoved the door open and pushed her way into the café, surprised to see half the customers crowding around the side windows, gasping, murmuring and muttering.

"Look at those teeth!" one voice shouted.

Another cried, "The baby!"

When a third yelled, "That animal is going to eat him alive," Abbie handed the tray off to Shannon.

"Any idea what's going on?" she asked.

Shannon shrugged. "No, something about a wolf."

"Wolf?" Abbie's voice went up several octaves. No wonder half the place was gathered around the window. Rubberneckers were nothing new to big cities or small towns. She spun around and stormed toward the door. "I'm going to see for myself what the heck is going on."

"I wouldn't worry," Donna called to her. "Jamie's on it."

The words "Jamie" and "wolf" so close together had Abbie hurrying out the door twice as fast as she'd intended. Careening around the corner past the new food tent, she pushed through the mulling crowds. When her gaze landed on Jamie stepping forward and both legs flying out from under him, her heart skipped a beat. As he landed flat on his back, she couldn't stop the scream that burst from deep in her lungs.

"Brooks!" one of the Farradays yelled. Not a calm 'hey brother' but a more urgent 'where the hell are you' tone.

Someone in the crowd cried out, "he's bleeding," and Abbie's gaze immediately landed on the large red pool beside his head.

This time it was Jamie's name that tore from her throat as she nearly catapulted over the remaining people lolling about. Sliding to the ground beside him, she took in his pale color and the surrounding puddle, not of blood, but ketchup. Only when she saw his eyelids fluttering did she take a real breath. Even so, he wasn't actually opening his eyes and that had her worrying still. A lot.

A hand on his cousin's shoulder, Adam was on one knee. "Can you hear me, Jamie?"

Tears pressed against her eyes. "Jamie," she said, more shakily than she'd wanted to. Her hand gently stroking his cheek. "Don't do this to me."

His eyelids fluttered again.

Both her hands enfolded his in hers. "Jamie," her voice came out high pitched and squeaky.

"What happened?" Brooks dropped to bended knee, edging his brother Adam aside.

"Did a ninja somersault saving Brittany from Gray," Adam started.

Pulling a pen light from his pocket, Brooks cast a quick are-you-kidding-me glance in his brother's direction. "Gray?"

"Yeah, I know that and you know that but Jamie's never seen either of the dogs. But what got him was the ketchup spill and a wayward puppy. The combo sent him flying."

Brooks flashed the light in Jamie's eye. "How long has he been out?"

"He," Jamie muttered, "is right here."

"Oh, thank God." Abbie blew out a relieved breath, tightening her grip on his hand.

"Where are we?" Brooks timed his patient's heart rate.

"You mean Tuckers Bluff, or the café, or were you referring to the more existential existence of this mortal life?"

Brooks rolled his eyes. "Apparently you didn't hit your head hard enough. Still, to be sure, I want to do a more thorough check in my office."

Still hanging onto his hand, Abbie nodded. "I'm coming with you."

Jamie lifted his eyes to meet hers. "Don't look so worried."

"Of course I'm worried. The man I love almost killed himself over ketchup."

Eyebrows squeezing his forehead, Jamie's eyes circled round. "You love me?"

"Oh, uh." This wasn't the way any reasonable woman would plan to tell a man that she was in love with him. "Maybe?" She smiled sheepishly.

His head lolled back and squeezing her hand, he smiled. "Close enough. And it's a good thing because I love you too."

Whether the eruption of applause around her was because of the declarations of love or the fact that he was awake and all right, Abbie didn't know, but right now, nothing in this world could be any sweeter than loving a man who loved her back.

• • • •

The last thing Jamie wanted was to be stuck alone in a doctor's office. Even if the doctor was his cousin Brooks. Any other day and he'd want to be back at the cafe or the parking lot battling it out for his pub. Except today wasn't any day. Today was the day Abbie said she loved him. And in front of witnesses.

"Good news is you're going to live." Brooks turned off the light on the x-ray reading panel.

"I could have told you that." He rubbed at the back of his neck. "Except for a bump on the head and a bruised ego for making a fool of myself over the town mascots, I'm healthy as a horse."

"And I hear," Brooks looked down his nose at Jamie, "in love too."

"Yes." His cheeks almost hurt from smiling.

"Good thing, cause she and half the family have been out in the lobby pacing."

"Only half?" Jamie teased.

"The other half has been keeping up with the cook-off."

His reality smacked him upside the head. "Speaking of which,

I need to get back."

"Not today you don't. That knot on your head means aspirin, nothing stressful, and someone nearby to keep an eye on you for at least twenty-four hours."

"That would be me." His aunt came through the door. "Cook-off is officially over."

Meg followed her. "Some of the shops are staying open a while longer taking advantage of the crowds."

"Frank is directing the cleanup," Becky reported.

"Frank?" Brooks frowned.

"Don't worry," Aunt Eileen waved at him. "He's doing it from a stool with his leg propped on a chair."

Most of the family filed in before Abbie finally appeared in the doorway. Sitting up on the exam table, he extended his arm to her.

"You sure know how to impress a girl, don't ya?" Taking his hand, she used her other one to brush a lock of hair away from his forehead. "Gives a whole new meaning to head over heels."

He used his free hand to rub the back of his neck. "Don't remind me."

Boot heels clicked down the hall, the sound arriving a few seconds before Grace appeared in the doorway. "I hear you put on quite the show today."

"I'm never going to live this down, am I?" Jamie asked.

All the voices in the room echoed, "No."

"I do come with news." Grace stepped further into the room. "I've conducted an informal exit poll of sorts. The council still doesn't have a majority to vote in favor of Farradays."

"So they're voting for Hemingway's?" Abbie asked, her grip on Jamie's hand tightening.

Abbie shook her head. "No one has enough of a majority."

"So we're back where we started," Jamie said softly.

"Not exactly." Grace leaned against the exam table and crossed her arms. "Seems Crocker and Hemingway's are going to withdraw their permit request and are no longer interested in buying property in Tuckers Bluff."

"You're kidding?" Jamie and Abbie chorused.

"Nope. Apparently, they saw with their own eyes what Jamie's been saying all along. This town, this county, is loyal to their own." One side of her smile lifted a little higher. "And it didn't hurt any when Stan Rankin , surrounded by three generations of one of the county's largest families, asked the lead rep to his face why in the name of all that was holy would they want to serve vegan burgers and eggplant bacon in meat eating cattle country?"

"Remind me to bake that man a blueberry pie," Aunt Eileen beamed. "Two."

Not caring who was watching, Jamie gave a tug of his wrist and pulled Abbie into the fold of his arms and planted a quick firm kiss smack on her lips. "We did it."

"Yes, well," Aunt Eileen cleared her throat, "I'd better go check on the cleanup."

"Good idea," Becky and Meg muttered simultaneously.

Aunt Eileen crossed the small room and pausing in front of Brooks, jabbed him in the side with her elbow.

"Ow." Brooks stared down at his aunt and quickly took a step back. "Yes, it's getting late. I think I'll take a minute here and call Joanna, see how she and Finn are doing with the baby."

All the visitors muttered polite conversation, proceeding out the office door in near military formation.

Jamie draped his arms around her waist. "Did you mean what you said out there?"

"*Don't do this to me*. Of course I did. My heart can't take much more loss in one lifetime."

"No," he shook his head, smiling at her. "The man I love part."

"Oh, that." Inching closer, she draped her arms over his shoulders. "Abso-love-you-lutely."

EPILOGUE

"Slainte," Sean and Brian Farraday toasted in unison. The packed house raised their glasses of beer, wine, water, cola, whatever was in front of them and echoed the celebratory call of 'to your health.'

"Ladies and gentlemen," the lead singer of the Irish band brought in from Austin for opening night of O'Fearadaigh's spoke into the mic. "We'd like to officially open the dance floor in this little bit of the old country here in Tuckers Bluff. Jamie, if you and your lovely lady would please come front and center."

Fortunately, every minute of the evening's events had been scheduled and orchestrated including this dance. From the moment he took Abbie's hand in his, their eyes locked on each other and the connection never broke. Not as she sat at the bar waiting for him to circle around, not when he took hold of her hand, not when they walked across the large room that felt as though it had been picked out of an Irish town and dropped in the middle of West Texas, and not while they moved around the dancefloor two stepping to an old Irish fiddle tune.

"They really are so well suited to each other." Meg Farraday watched her husband's cousin and her first friend in Tuckers Bluff glide around the floor.

"I'm not surprised." Eileen took a sip of her drink. "After all, the dogs haven't gotten it wrong yet." The rational part of her mind, the logical intelligent person in her knew there was no such thing as matchmaking dogs or their matchmaking offspring. But another part of her, perhaps the whimsical Irish side, really wanted to believe in the dogs' matchmaking skills.

Meg burst out laughing. "If that's true, I wonder who those other two puppies are for."

"Oh," Eileen tore her gaze away from her nephew and Abbie, "I hadn't thought of that." Scanning the packed pub, she spied Sally May and Roy sharing a booth. Even though the council never got the chance to vote on who got the permit for the license with only one application on file, Roy had been so sweet in asking Sally May to accompany him for opening night that she didn't have the heart to say no. "Who knew?"

"Huh?" Meg asked, following Eileen's gaze.

"Turns out Roy has had his eye on Sally May since high school. Back then he was too young for her. Now a few years don't seem to matter."

"Apparently not. They seem to be hitting it off now, and Old Octopus Arms is keeping his hands to himself."

Eileen nearly choked on her craft beer. "Where'd you hear that?" Poor man hadn't been able to live that name down since high school.

"I think from Abbie."

Shaking her head, Eileen set her drink on the table. "I'll admit in school he had a reputation for being a little too handy—if you know what I mean—but once his brains caught up to his hormones, he's been a fine upstanding citizen and his late wife Sharlene was the salt of the earth." Still, just in case, Eileen planned to keep an eye out for those other puppies.

The lead singer called for the audience to join in on the dance and chairs scraped against the hardwood floors as most of the folks around them joined in on the fun.

"It was a surprise to learn Abbie was closing the café tonight." Meg had been keeping a close eye on Jamie and her old boss.

"Not any more surprising than her hiring on a new waitress and taking three nights a week off." The minute Eileen had heard all the plans the two were making, she knew it wouldn't be long before there was a ring on Abbie's finger and another wedding to organize. Though frankly, she was a little surprised the ring hadn't already come. After all, neither of them was getting any younger.

Meg's phone dinged and from the bright smile that took over her face, Eileen was pretty sure who it was.

"Adam?"

"Yep. The Brady's have a new healthy calf and mama is doing fine. He's on his way home."

"Good. Plenty of time for two stepping."

"What about you? Surely there's a nice single man around who can give you a whirl around the floor?"

"Ha," Eileen scoffed. "That'll be the day."

"You never know." Meg shrugged. "The pub's going to bring a lot of changes to town. Good changes. Already bookings at the B&B are up."

"That is good news."

"Yes. Soon we may have to actually open a small hotel."

While a little economic growth was good for everyone, Eileen sure hoped things wouldn't change that much. She'd grown accustom to the perks of small town living. "I don't know that we'll bring in that many new people."

"Maybe not. But even now we've got a nice older guy staying with us. That doesn't happen often."

"Traveling alone?" Eileen asked. Meg was right, typically couples and families passed through town.

"Yeah, that surprised me. He's pretty good looking for his age. Likes to talk. His wife passed a couple of years ago. Not sure he's over her yet."

"What brings him to Tuckers Bluff? Surely not the pub?"

"Not really sure about that either. He said something about ghosts but I don't think he was referring to the ghost town trail, since except for meals, he's been mostly holed up in his room for a few days now."

"Maybe he and his late wife had something special about Tuckers Bluff?"

"Don't know. Got the impression he'd never been here before. I feel like this is his first trip to Texas."

The music came to a slow stop and the lights in the place

dimmed dramatically. Only the lights over the dance floor remained on. When the crowd separated, Eileen had a clear view of her nephew on bended knee and shot her hand out to Meg. "Oh, look."

The proverbial pin could have been heard falling to the ground.

"Abbie," Jamie cleared his throat, "I've waited a long time to find my better half. Would you do me the honor of making me the happiest man on the planet? Marry me?"

Eyes wide and right hand on her heart, Abbie bobbed her head, throwing her arms around his neck, toppling them both over onto the floor.

The crowd cheered and applauded. Eileen could barely hear what Jamie said next, but seated on the wooden dance floor he slipped a ring onto her finger and kissed her in front of half the town.

"That's just too sweet," Meg said on a sigh.

Eileen nodded, unable to stop grinning. Romance was alive and well in Tuckers Bluff.

The lights still dimmed, a ray of streetlight beamed into the pub. Eileen turned to the door and not till it closed behind the tall silhouette and the overhead lighting came back on did she see clearly who had come inside. At first she thought she must have had one beer too many except she hadn't finished her first. By the time he'd made his way a few more feet inside, Eileen was sure he was no hallucination. "Of all the gin joints in all the towns in all the world…"

MEET CHRIS

USA TODAY Bestselling Author of more than a dozen contemporary novels, including the award winning *Champagne Sisterhood*, Chris Keniston lives in suburban Dallas with her husband, two human children, and two canine children. Though she loves her puppies equally, she admits being especially attached to her German Shepherd rescue. After all, even dogs deserve a happily ever after.

More on Chris and her books can be found at
www.chriskeniston.com

Follow Chris on Facebook at ChrisKenistonAuthor
or on Twitter @ckenistonauthor

Questions? Comments?
I would love to hear from you.
You can reach me at chris@chriskeniston.com

82310151R00093

Made in the USA
San Bernardino, CA
14 July 2018